DEADLY EDGE

After a smooth and complex robbery is carried out by Parker and three associates, a corpse is discovered at the hideout. Someone is trying to find Parker and the other members of the gang, and those who are found don't survive the meeting. Parker leaves his woman, Claire, to hunt the hunters, following a brutal and twisted trail that leads him right back to Claire, now a hostage to as evil a pair as has ever been imagined . . .

DEADLY EDGE

Richard Stark

ATLANTIC LARGE PRINT

Chivers Press, Bath, England.
Curley Publishing, Inc.,
South Yarmouth, Mass., USA.

Library of Congress Cataloging-in-Publication Data

Stark, Richard.
    Deadly edge / Richard Stark.
        p.   cm.—(Atlantic large print)
    ISBN 0–7927–1102–5 (softcover)
    1. Large type books.   I. Title.
[PS3573.E9D43   1992]
823′.914—dc20   91–36716
                                                                        CIP

British Library Cataloguing in Publication Data available

This Large Print edition is published by Chivers Press, England, and
Curley Publishing, Inc, U.S.A. 1992

Published by arrangement with the author

U.K. Hardback ISBN 0 7451 8354 9
U.K. Softback ISBN 0 7451 8366 2
U.S.A. Softback ISBN 0 7927 1102 5

This is for Joe Gores,
for the hell of it

DEADLY EDGE

PART ONE

CHAPTER ONE

Up here, the music was just a throbbing under the feet, a distant pulse. Down below, down through the roof, through and beneath the offices, down in the amphitheater shaped like a soup bowl, the crowd was roaring and pounding and yelling down at the four musicians in the bottom of the bowl. The musicians scooped up the roars coming in at them, pushed them through electric guitars and amplifiers, and sent back howls of sound that dwarfed the noise of the crowd, till the roaring was like a blast of heat on the face. But up here it was no more than a continuing throb in the gravelly surface of the roof.

Parker raised the ax over his head and swung it hard down into the tarred surface of the roof. *Thop* went the ax. Parker and the two men beside him heard clearly the sound of the ax, but even as close by as the man on lookout at the fire escape, the sound was lost.

'That'll take all night,' Keegan said, but Keegan was a nay-sayer and no one ever listened to him.

Parker lifted the ax again, swung it again, twisted it slightly as it struck, and this time a touch of more amber color showed through the tar and gravel: wood.

Parker moved to the left, so his next slice

3

would be across the first two, and lifted the ax again. He was a big man, blocky and wide, with heavy hands roped across the backs with veins. His head was square, ears flat to the skull, hair thin and black. His face had a bony rough-cut look, as though the sculptor hadn't come back to do the final detail work. He was wearing black sneakers, black permanent-press slacks, and a black zippered nylon jacket; the jacket was reversible, a light blue on the other side, and under it he was wearing a white shirt and a blue-and-gold tie. Cheap brown cotton work gloves were on his hands, and on the hands of the other three.

It was spring, a dry but cloudy night, the temperature in the low fifties. It was ten minutes past midnight; down below, the Saturday midnight show was building toward crescendo. The final show at the old Civic Auditorium. Monday the wreckers would arrive. From up here on the roof, the poured-concrete flying-saucer shape of the new auditorium could be seen on Urban Renewal-cleared land half a dozen blocks away.

Keegan said, 'I don't like it up here.' A stocky man, just under average height, Keegan had thick dry brown hair and the outraged expression of a barroom arguer. He, too, was dressed in dark clothing; he kept forgetting about the gloves on his hands, starting to put his hands in his pockets—each time he would suddenly remember, look startled, and then shake his head in irritation with himself.

Each time Parker swung the ax now, more wood showed. There was over an inch of tarpaper and tar and stones on top of the wood, and the ax blade was getting streaked black with tar. After half a dozen swings with the ax, Parker had exposed a chopped-up section of wood about the size and shape of a footprint. After his seventh swing, Briley said, 'Let me have a whack at it,' and Parker handed over the ax and stepped back out of the way.

Briley was tall, but lean, and spoke with the hill accent of Tennessee. His face was deeply lined, more than it should have been in a man his age, and the lines were black, as though they'd been drawn on with charcoal. Briley had been two things earlier in his life—fat and a miner—but since the nine days he'd spent underground after a cave-in, he'd been neither. He swung the ax now hard and mean, as though it were Appalachia he was chopping.

Parker stood and watched, his hands dangling loose at his sides. When in motion, he looked tough and determined and fast, but when waiting, when at rest, he looked inert and lifeless.

Keegan went over to talk to Morris, the man sitting on the low wall at the edge of the roof, his arm carelessly draped over the curving top rail of the fire escape. Parker could hear the querulous sound of Keegan's voice, but not the words. Morris, a young, soft-looking man with slumped shoulders, was also their driver. His quiet nondescript voice filled the small spaces left by Keegan's. Morris had the calm and even temper of a man who doesn't care about anything. He was a pothead, and he'd dabbled in the harder drugs, but not while working; Parker had made sure of that ahead of time.

Briley made a dozen fast mean slashes at the roof with the ax, extending the area of the chopped-up exposed wood to about the size of a mess-hall tin, and then Parker called, 'Keegan, come take your turn.'

'I'm coming.' Even that sounded querulous.

Morris sat up straighter on the wall and called, 'You want me to take a turn?'

'You just keep an eye down below.'

'Somebody else could watch for me.'

'It's better to keep one man on watch,' Parker said, and turned his back so Morris wouldn't argue any more. He'd learned long ago that in dealing with men, it was always best to curb impatience and give them explanations, but he'd also learned that explanations could go on forever if they weren't cut off.

Briley took one more hack at the roof, then

6

reluctantly turned over the ax to Keegan. Stepping back, grinning, wiping his forehead with the back of one hand, Briley said, 'That's a good workout.'

Keegan hesitated a minute, holding the ax across his body at thigh-height with both hands, making sure he had his feet set right. But he swung hard and clear, and he knew to twist the handle as the blade went in.

After the first stroke, he said, 'We'll be at this till morning.' The next swing, the ax blade sank on through the wood and almost knocked him off-balance.

'Hold it,' Parker said. Keegan pulled the ax out and stood back watching, and Parker went down on one knee beside the hole. He took off his right glove and picked away some splinters of wood, then felt around underneath with the tips of his fingers. Nodding, he got to his feet again and said, 'There's a space under. Chop the hole a little bigger, but don't go straight down. We don't know about wiring.'

Keegan bent over the hole, gripping the ax near the blade with his right hand and halfway down the handle with his left. Using short chops, he sliced away at the gouged wood, opening a hole the size of a coffee-container lid, then stopped.

'Bigger than that,' Parker said. 'We've got to be able to see in there.'

'I think I'm hitting a two-by-twelve here on

the right. I'll go the other way.'

The other three watched him, and Keegan bent low over his work, chopping six inches from his feet. He opened a hole as big around as a guard's hat, and then stepped back again.

'I'll get the flashlight,' Briley said. There were two metal toolkits on the roof out of the way, and Briley went to them and opened the one on the left.

Parker went down on one knee again, picked away the splinters from around the edge of the hole, and when Briley brought him the flashlight he bent low over the hole to shield the light while he looked inside.

The tar had been laid down on tarpaper, which had been tacked to wooden planks. The planks, Parker now saw, had been laid across two-by-twelve joists sixteen inches apart. A ceiling of planks was fastened across the underpart of the joists, closing this space off. There was neither electric wiring nor insulation anywhere to be seen.

Parker switched off the flashlight and got to his feet. 'I think we've got an extra level to go through.'

'There's always some damn thing,' Keegan said.

'I can use the workout,' Briley said.

Parker took the ax and took full swings, clearing the tar out of a wider area, bounded by the joists underneath. Keegan went back over to complain to Morris some more, but

8

Briley stood impatiently waiting for Parker to be finished with his turn at the ax.

Briley ended the job at this level, swiping the ax down sideways, as though playing golf, stripping wood away even with the joist-edge on both sides. Then he and Parker pulled all the shards and splinters out of the hole.

Briley said, 'That wood'll be nothing to punch out.'

'We don't know what's under it. Hold the light for me.'

From the toolkits Parker got a hand drill and a narrow handsaw. He and Briley knelt across the hole from each other, and while Briley held the flashlight low, Parker drilled a hole in the planking near one of the joists, put the drill to one side, inserted the first few inches of the saw into the hole, and slowly sawed the one plank all the way across. Then Briley got a hammer and chisel, and while Parker held the light, he pried up one edge across the saw-mark. His hands around the edge of the plank, knees braced on the roof, Briley bent the plank upward and back until it cracked with a sound like a pistol shot in a barn.

'Got you, you son of a bitch.'

Grinning, Briley twisted the plank back and forth till it ripped entirely free. Keegan had come back over by now, and the three of them looked down in when Parker shone the light through the new hole. They saw fluffy

9

pinkness, like clouds: insulation. Also a length of old-fashioned metal-shielded electric cable.

Keegan said, 'Now where do you suppose the box is?' Electricity was his department.

Parker said, 'We'll have to assume it's live.'

Briley said, 'At least the saw won't cut through it. I saw a boy do that once with the new wire.'

'It wouldn't hurt him,' Keegan said. 'Your saw handles are wood.'

Briley demonstrated with hand gestures, saying, 'He had his left hand on the top of the saw for more pressure.' He grinned and said, 'There's a boy burned for his sins.'

'Kill him?' Keegan sounded really interested.

'No. Threw him about twelve foot.'

Parker began to saw again. After a while he gave the saw to Keegan, and in the silence before Keegan started, the music could be heard, very faintly. But an actual presence now, and not merely a vibration.

As each plank was sawn through, Briley gripped it, bent it up and back, and each one snapped near the opposite joist. When an area had been cleared about a foot square, Parker took a linoleum knife from one of the toolkits and used it to cut through the insulation, slicing across the same line over and over until he got down to the paper backing. He slit that across, reached his gloved fingers

10

under, and ripped the insulation upward. It had been stapled to the joists on both sides, and came up in a series of quick jerks.

And underneath was sheetrock, which should be the ceiling of the room below. The surfaces, from top to bottom, were the tar and gravel on tarpaper on wood laid across joists set on wooden planks laid across more joists going in the opposite direction, against the bottom of which was the sheetrock. With the joists, vertical two-by-twelve beams, going one way in the top air space and the other way in the lower insulated airspace, that meant there would be no opening they could make larger than fifteen inches square.

It was twelve-thirty when Parker took the linoleum knife and began to score the sheetrock along the edge of one joist; they'd been at this twenty minutes. They'd opened an area larger than they'd be able to use, and the electric cable was just outside the section they were working on.

Parker scored the sheetrock three times down the same line, and the fourth time the knife broke through over the whole length. Briley was holding the flashlight again now; Parker dropped the knife on the sheetrock and got to his feet, saying to Keegan, 'I did the left side.'

Keegan got down on his knees beside the hole. 'Getting colder,' he commented, though it wasn't, and went to work on the opposite

11

side. When that was cut through, he scored a line bridging the cuts at one end, drew the knife down along that line again, and when he did it a third time, the whole section of sheetrock sagged downward.

Parker had been standing across from Keegan, watching. Now he said, 'We want to lift it up, if we can.'

Keegan looked up, squinting into darkness after looking into the flashlight's illumination. 'Why not just kick it through?'

'Noise.'

'Who'd hear anything with that racket? That's the whole idea, isn't it?' Every time they removed a layer of roof, the music and the crowd noises get louder. Now it was at about the level of a busy country bar on Saturday night, as heard from the driveway.

'We don't know if there's a room under this one,' Parker said. 'Or if anybody's in it. They'd hear something that heavy hit the floor.'

'No problem, anyway,' Briley said, squatting down beside the hole. 'Here, hold the flash, Keegan.'

Keegan took the flashlight, and Briley took the linoleum knife. He chipped away a little at the stationary part of the end-line, so there'd be room for his fingers, then put the linoleum knife to one side, reached down to grasp the end of the sagging section of the sheetrock, and pulled it slowly upward. It curved, but wouldn't split.

Parker stood beside him and took one corner in both hands. 'Get a better grip.'

'Thanks.' Briley, still holding the sheetrock, got to his feet and then shifted his hands to the other corner. 'When you're ready.'

They pulled upward, and the sheetrock cracked along the fourth side with a flat sound like two pool balls hitting. They leaned it back at an angle against the edge of the cleared section, like an open trapdoor.

Morris called, 'Something happening down below.'

All three went over to look. They were about fifty feet from the ground, the equivalent of a six-story building. There were windows in the top two stories, but below that the wall was blank. Black metal doors led out to the fire escape on the top two landings. By day, the wall was made of grimy gray-tan bricks; by night, it was simply darkness, with an illuminated blacktop alley at the bottom. Down there, near the bottom of the fire escape, a pair of large black metal doors led inside somewhere; all equipment for the shows put on here came through the wrought-iron gates at the sidewalk end of the alley, down across the blacktop and through those metal doors. At the far end, the alley was stopped by a blank brick wall. The opposite side of the alley was the rear wall of the Strand, a shut-down movie theater. The Strand and the Civic Auditorium stood back to back at opposite ends of a long block, all of which would come down, starting Monday. A sixty-eight-story office building covering the whole block was due to go up, starting next year.

Down below now, the wrought-iron gates over by the sidewalk were standing half-open, and someone was moving around with flashlights. Two of them, with two flashlights.

'Now how the hell did they get on to us?' Keegan said. He didn't sound surprised.

'They're not onto us,' Morris said. He was still sitting on the wall, half-twisted around, with his shoulder braced against the curving top rail of the fire escape as he looked down.

'They're cops, though,' Briley said.

'Looking for groupies,' Morris said.

Keegan turned an exasperated frown on Morris. Things he didn't understand he liked even less than things he did understand. 'Groupies? What the hell's a groupie?'

'Rock-and-roll fan. Mostly girls.'

Briley laughed and said, 'Looking for autographs?'

'Looking to get laid.'

A flashlight beam arched upward in their direction, and they all leaned backward. They waited a few seconds, and then Morris took a look and said, 'They're all done.'

'Just so they don't come up the fire escape,'

Keegan said.

Parker looked over the edge, and the flashlights were moving back toward the wrought-iron gates.

Morris said, 'Just an easy check. Now they'll put a man outside the gates, so nobody climbs over.'

'By God,' said Keegan irritably, 'what if they see something on the Strand door?'

They wouldn't, because there was nothing to see, but nobody bothered to answer him.

They had gotten here through the Strand. At four-thirty this afternoon they'd driven up to the entrance of the Strand in a gray-and-white Union Electric Company truck, all four of them wearing gray one-piece coveralls with the company name in white on the back. It had been simple to get through the lobby doors of the Strand, carrying three toolkits, the third containing sandwiches and a Thermos container of coffee. Briley and Keegan and Morris had played blackjack to pass the time, betting the expected proceeds from this job, but Parker had slept for a while, walked around the dusty-smelling empty theater for a while, and sat for a while in darkness in the manager's office, looking out at the city. He'd watched the crowds form for the early show, all the bright colors after the gray centuries of Reason, and then the traffic. Then he'd left the office to walk some more.

15

He had a woman, named Claire, that he found himself thinking about while waiting. She was somewhere in the Northeast now, buying a house; the thought of having a woman who owned a house was a strange one. He'd been married once, to a woman named Lynn, but they'd lived in hotels; his life, and she'd adapted to it. She was dead now; she'd been hard, but pressure had come to her, and she'd broken. The new one, Claire, was not hard, but Parker thought she wouldn't break.

Morris said, 'There they go,' and the wrought-iron gates closed, and there was no longer any light down there except the one yellow globe suspended from a metal pipe jutting out of the Civic Auditorium wall. 'I doubt they'll be back.'

Parker said, 'Watch. Just in case.'

'Oh, I will.'

Parker and Briley and Keegan went back to the hole they'd made and squatted down on their haunches, and Briley shone the flashlight down into the room below.

So far, the map they'd bought had been absolutely right. Right about the Strand, the alley, the fire escape, the roof. And now, right about the room. They'd chopped where the map said to chop, and it had led them to an empty office. 'Public Relations,' the map had told them; 'already moved to temporary offices in another building.'

Sometimes jobs were done this way, from a

16

map—a package, really, like a do-it-yourself radio kit—bought from a middleman who had bought it from someone on the inside, a non-professional who simply laid out the particulars of the case. Years before, most of John Dillinger's jobs had been done that way, bought as a packet from a middleman, and it was still sometimes the best way to get set up.

The office below was just as the map had described: medium size, two desks, four chairs, a short brown Naugahyde sofa, several gray-metal filing cabinets. One of the desks, empty except for a green blotter, black telephone and one wrinkled legal-sized envelope, was directly beneath the hole.

'Hold this,' Briley said. Parker took the flashlight from him, and Briley put both hands on one of the lower-level joists and dropped down into the room. He swung forward once, backward once, and dropped two feet to the desk top. He grinned up toward the flashlight and dropped lithely down to the gray carpet.

Behind each of the desks was a swivel chair; beside each desk was a straight armless wooden chair. Briley now picked up the nearest wooden chair and put it on top of the desk. 'Join me.'

Keegan went next, more awkwardly than Briley, having trouble at first finding his footing on the chair. Briley held the chair steady, but didn't touch Keegan, who got his balance, released the joist over his head, held the chair back instead, and stepped down onto the desk. He sat down on the desk, put his feet over the side, and stood up on the floor, dusting white sheetrock powder from the seat of his pants.

Parker called to Morris, 'Going down now.'

'Have a good time.'

Parker dropped the flashlight to Briley, who lit his way. He dropped to the chair, jumped to the desk, then to the floor.

'This is the worst time,' Keegan said. 'Right now. What would we do if that door opened and a lot of cops came in?'

Neither of the other two said anything. Keegan had lost over four hundred dollars he didn't have yet in the blackjack game: two hundred fifty to Briley, the rest to Morris. It had made him more pessimistic and irritable than usual.

This room had a window, but it opened on a narrow airshaft that came up the middle of the building. The top of the airshaft had been their landmark on the roof. Since the door was solid wood, there was no reason not to turn the light on. Briley went over and flicked the wall switch by the door, and put away the flashlight. He said, 'Now we make our stairway. To paradise, huh?'

'Listen to that music,' Keegan said peevishly. 'What the hell ever happened to jazz?'

18

'It's still there,' Briley said, going over to the filing cabinets, 'in the same gin mills it always was. When did jazz ever play a joint like this?'

'Jazz at the Phil,' Keegan said. 'I used to have all those records, before that time I got sent up.'

'Jazz at the Phil,' Briley said scornfully. 'Fake.' He opened a file drawer. 'Empty! There's a break.'

'What do you mean, fake? All the greats were on *Jazz at the Phil.*'

'Okay,' Briley said. 'Give us a hand here, will you?'

Keegan went over to help him move the filing cabinet. 'I don't know how you can call them a fake. My God! Lester Hawkins, Dizzy Gillespie, Johnny Hodges—'

'I guess you're right,' Briley said, grinning. 'I must of been thinking of something else.'

Parker had taken the chair down off the desk, and now stood at one end of it. Briley and Keegan put the filing cabinet down, picked up the other end of the desk, and the three of them moved it over till it was no longer directly beneath the hole. Then Briley and Keegan moved the filing cabinet to abut against the edge of the desk closest to the hole, while Parker put the chair back up on top of the desk again. They kept moving furniture, and when they were done they had a complicated stairway leading up toward the

19

hole, and facing the doorway. A man coming in the doorway would have two or three strides into the room, then a foot-high step to an upended metal wastebasket, then a step a foot and a half high to the desk, another foot and a half up to the wooden chair, a foot to the top of three filing cabinets lined up in a row, and finally a foot and a half to the second wooden chair, on top of the filing cabinets. This put one six and a half feet above the floor, where the top of the roof came to about waist-level; an easy climb. This kind of stairway was better in two ways then any kind of rope ladder or anything of that sort they might have brought with them; first, because it meant one less thing they had to carry to the job, and second, because it could be gone up faster than any kind of portable ladder.

Briley now went up their staircase and out onto the roof, and Parker went partway up after him. Briley handed down the toolkits one at a time to Parker, who handed them down to Keegan. Briley said something to Morris, waved, and came back down into the room.

Keegan had already opened the other toolkit. The three masks he removed from it were made of black cotton and covered the entire head, with openings for eyes and mouth. The three handguns were all Smith & Wesson Model .39's, a 9mm Luger automatic with an eight-shot clip. There were also three small blue packets: blue plastic laundry bags, costing a nickel each from a laundromat vending machine.

They put on the masks and checked their guns and stowed the little laundry-bag packages in their pockets. Then Parker nodded to Briley, who flicked off the light switch and in darkness opened the door.

There was some light in the hall outside, not much. But much more noise. Whenever the music ended, the crowd noise increased to a kind of ecstatic scream, fading as the music started up again, but gradually building through the next number till music and crowd seemed about equally matched by the end of the tune, when there would be another concerted scream.

It was five past one; they'd been working fifty-five minutes since Parker first swung the ax into the roof.

Parker was the first into the hall, looking to the right and left. Doors on both sides of the hall in both directions, mostly closed, a few standing open. No lights burning up at this level at all. Far down to the right a stairwell, with light shining up, reflecting off the pale green corridor walls, giving light to see by down here.

Parker turned right, and the other two followed, Briley turning the doorknob to be sure the lock wasn't on, then shutting the door behind them. Keegan carried the one

21

toolkit they still needed.

The flooring was some sort of composition, similar to linoleum; the sneakers they wore made no sounds against it. They walked slowly, leaning slightly forward, their right hands holding the automatics ahead of them and out away from their bodies.

If Morris saw trouble coming now, they were past the point where they could retrace their steps. Morris's job would be to come in after them and let them know their primary exit was blocked; they had a second exit route planned for, and a third.

The noise was coming up the stairwell almost undiluted by distance. Standing at the top, looking over the rail and down at six flights of brightly lit empty silent metal stairs, hearing the rush of sound coming up there and yet not seeing any living person, you could begin to stop hearing the music as music, but simply as noise. Then it became the workings of some gigantic machine in a pit in the earth, and men who went down into it were chewed and ground and mangled.

'Jesus,' Keegan said. Looking out the eyeholes of the mask, his eyes looked frightened; not by the job they were here to do, but by the noise that was supposed to cover them while they did it.

Parker started down the stairs. Briley came second, and Keegan third.

The walls were plaster, and painted pale

green. The stairs had a landing and a U-turn halfway down every flight. At the top floor the stairs had been open, but at the next level down there was a wall, with a green metal fire door. A darker green than the walls. The door was closed.

Parker put his hand on the knob and waited for the other two to come down to him. Then, quickly, he opened the door and stepped through.

One of the notes with the map had said: 'One private guard in the hall—armed—always watches show.' He was there, he was watching the show, he never saw Parker and the other two come in at all.

On this floor, there were offices along one side of the corridor only, opposite the stairwell entrance. The other side of the corridor had sections of plate glass at intervals, through which could be seen the main soup bowl of the auditorium. The ceiling of the auditorium, barnacled with lighting equipment, was just above these plate-glass windows, giving the impression that one was viewing from above the auditorium rather than from within it—for the Caesar effect.

It was at one of these windows that the guard was standing. A thin and potbellied man in his fifties, wearing a gray uniform with a gold circular patch on the sleeve, a wood-handled revolver in a holster high up

23

toward the waist on his right side, he was standing there with his hands clasped behind him, head bent forward and down, face in a relaxed expression of blank attention, as though he were daydreaming under cover of the noise. With only space and the one sheet of glass in the way, the sound volume here was very loud, much louder even than in the stairwell.

Parker walked down the corridor toward the guard, Keegan to his left and Briley to his right, forming a triangle shape that filled the width of the hall. They were halfway from the stairwell entrance before their movement attracted the guard's attention; then he made a startled automatic move toward his revolver. But it was too high on his waist—he'd put it there for the comfort of his potbelly, no doubt—and a leather strap was snapped in place over the top of the holster to keep the revolver from falling out, and the three faceless men walking toward him all had guns already in their hands. And there was no furniture, no handy open doorway, no place to run, no cover to hide behind; nothing but the empty hallway. The guard, looking bitter and angry and disgusted, straightened from the half-crouch he'd naturally moved into, and slowly lifted his hands over his head.

'Put them down,' Parker said. The guard didn't make out the words through the noise, so Parker went closer and said again, 'Put your hands down. Leave them at your sides. Now walk toward us.' When the guard was no longer in front of the glass, Parker said, 'Now stop. Turn left. Put your hands on the wall in front of you at head-height. Lean forward. Touch your forehead to the wall.'

The guard managed as far as touching his hatbrim to the wall. Briley came forward and took the revolver out of the holster, having to use two hands to unsnap the leather strap. He put the revolver away in his hip pocket, and took his own automatic out again, then stepped back a pace.

Parker said, 'All right. Straighten up. Turn around. Good.'

Briley took the two-way radio from the guard's left shirt pocket and backed up next to Parker again. The guard was looking more disgusted by the second.

Parker said, 'What's your name?'

The guard frowned at him, not understanding the reason for the question, but he answered it: 'Dockery.'

'First name.'

'Patrick.'

'Do they call you Patrick or Pat?'

'When it's bums like you,' the guard said bitterly, 'they call me Mr. Dockery.'

Briley, grinning, said, 'Ah, Paddy Dockery, you talk mighty big when it's three against one. You know you're safe from us. I'd like to see you in a fair fight.'

Dockery gave him a brooding look. 'You'll laugh out of the other side of your face,' he said.

'All right, Dockery,' Parker said. 'Turn around. Walk slowly to the men's room.'

The four of them made a small silent procession, out of phase with the beat of the music surrounding them. Dockery passed four doors on his left side, and turned toward the fifth, reaching his hand out to the knob.

Parker said, 'If you open that door, I'll kill you and everybody the other side of it. I said the men's room.'

Dockery's hand hesitated, an inch from the knob. His shoulders were tensed to reject the bullet, but in the end he leaned back from the door and his hand dropped to his side. Not turning to look at Parker, he said, 'It's not my own life I was thinking of.'

'I know that,' Parker said. This was one of his specialties, as electricity was one of Keegan's specialties and driving was one of Morris's. Rare is the high-number robbery that isn't cluttered up with people—bank customers or armored-car guards or store clerks or whatever. One of Parker's specialties was handling the people, which meant keeping them quiet, making sure none of them got killed, making sure none of them loused up the routine. The last was the most important, and the others would be sacrificed to it, if necessary, though a neat job was

26

always better.

Parker was now handling the person called Patrick Dockery. Dockery was a proud and prickly man, and what he would be feeling now was mostly humiliation. He was the kind who would take almost any sort of damn-fool risk, would even throw his life away, to erase humiliation. He would open the wrong door, he might even turn and attack three armed men. He had to be handled until he'd been successfully maneuvered into the privacy of the men's room, where he could be physically restrained. Out here in the hall, it meant giving him his respect back, easing his sense of humiliation. By letting him wise off, and by acknowledging that it really had been other people's lives he'd been thinking of when he'd moved his hand back from that doorknob. Parker was treating his foolhardiness as though it were worthy of respect; if he had judged his man right, Dockery would respond by being good and doing what he was told.

As he did. He led them now to the right room, and all four trooped inside, around the green metal wall divider just inside the door and into the main open green-tiled square of the room itself, where Parker said, 'Take off the uniform.'

There was no way around this. The humiliation was harsh and blatant, but it was necessary.

27

Dockery turned around, and there were pale circles of strain around his eyes. 'You go to hell,' he said.

'You aren't going to stop us,' Parker told him. 'Don't make things tougher for yourself.'

Dockery glared a second longer, and then suddenly ran backward away from them, his head back and mouth open, shoving the first two fingers of his right hand down his throat.

'Damn it!' Briley jumped forward like a steeplechaser, swinging hard and fast with the automatic, the way he'd swung the ax earlier up on the roof. The barrel clipped Dockery on the forearm, near the wrist, and Dockery instinctively moved the arm, his hand no longer near his mouth. His hat had fallen off, and Briley kicked it to the side, then lunged forward, punching his shoulder into Dockery's chest and running him backward the rest of the way into the wall, where he hit the side edge of a urinal, half-turned, and hit his left shoulder and the side of his head against the tile wall. Briley held him pinned there at arm's length, his hand flat with splayed fingers on Dockery's chest, as with the toe of his right shoe he started angrily kicking Dockery's shins. 'Son of a bitch,' he said, kicking at Dockery's legs. 'Stupid-ass son of a bitch.'

Parker came up beside them and said, 'Stop that.' The music was down to a usable

28

level again in here; he could talk in a normal tone of voice.

Briley stopped the kicking, but kept holding Dockery jammed against the wall. Turning his head, he complained, 'He was gonna throw up on his uniform! I got to *wear* that uniform!'

'That was his idea,' Parker said.

'He thinks he's smart.' Briley was panting and enraged. Glaring at Dockery through the eyeholes of his mask, he said, 'Gonna screw up our plan, not let me wear the uniform. You know what kind of smart that is? That's *stupid* smart!'

Parker leaned close to look at Dockery, who seemed dazed and winded and in pain. Parker said, 'If you cause us any more trouble, I don't answer for what he'll do to you.'

Dockery blinked at him, still mutinous. 'I'll remember you people.'

'That you will,' Briley said. He abruptly pulled his hand away from Dockery's chest and stepped back a pace, and Dockery almost fell, but grabbed the urinal and held himself up till he got his balance back.

'Take off your tie,' Parker said, and when Dockery didn't move at once, Briley yelled, 'Damn it, I'll kick you into hamburger, I swear to God I will!'

Parker, still looking at Dockery, said to Briley, 'That's enough. He'll do it. He wants

29

to be in shape to identify us at the line-up.'

It was the right approach, at last. Dockery almost smiled, and there was less mutiny and more strength in his voice when he said, 'And you'll be there, don't you worry. And I wouldn't miss it for the world.' With a sudden angry gesture, as though it were an act of defiance, he reached up and yanked down on the knot of his tie, pulling the tie loose and flinging it with a contemptuous underhand flip toward Briley, who caught it in midair and said, 'Do me a favor. Hang by your thumbs till we show up.'

Keegan, who had stayed over by the door in case anyone else should come in, the toolkit at the floor by his feet, now called, 'What's taking so long? We don't have all night.'

'We're ahead of schedule,' Parker called to him. They didn't have that specific a schedule, but he didn't want Dockery to get the idea he could fight them some more by moving very slowly.

As it was, Dockery was slow enough. Briley took each piece of clothing as it was tossed at him, and stood there with the parts of uniform over one arm. He wasn't naturally a cruel man, and by the time Dockery got to his trousers Briley had cooled off and was no longer angry. Dockery had fresh jagged cuts on both shins, the skin around the cuts ragged like wrinkled onion-skin paper,

30

droplets of blood oozing to the surface of the cuts. The trousers were the last, and when Briley had them he stood there a couple of seconds looking at Dockery's legs, and then said, in a muted voice, 'I'm sorry I did that.'

'You will be,' Dockery said. His face was tight and unforgiving.

'I got mad, is all,' Briley explained, apologizing again.

Dockery didn't bother to answer that. He turned his head to look at Parker, accepting him as the leader and waiting to be told what to do next.

Parker said, 'Go over to the first stall.'

Dockery was in his underwear, socks, and shoes. Somehow he had more dignity now, not less. Out of the uniform, more of his own individuality was apparent; he looked less potbellied, and less ineffective. He seemed to sense the change in his appearance himself, and to behave accordingly; he strode over to the stall without fuss, without either defiance or defeat.

Briley had gone into another stall to change. Keegan came over to watch Dockery while Parker put his automatic away, took the handcuffs from his left hip pocket, got Dockery seated in the stall, and handcuffed his hands behind him, the cuff chain running under the pipe that came out of the wall about thirty inches from the ground. Dockery would be fairly comfortable there, but wouldn't be able to get away.

Parker stepped back out of the stall and was about to pull the metal door shut when Dockery called, 'Hey.' Parker looked at him, and Dockery said, 'I don't want any of you killed. I want you captured alive. I want to be able to testify against you, and I want to be able to see your faces. I want you to get sent up. I want to know that you'll be getting years of what you gave me tonight.'

'It may happen,' Parker said, and shut the stall door.

Briley was coming out, in the uniform and without his mask. The pants were a little too short, and too big around the waist, but the shortness just made him look like an old man, and the gunbelt disguised the excess material at the waist.

Briley's taking the guard's part was a last-minute change in the routine. An old man named Berridge had originally been set to do it. There'd been three meetings to set things up, and at the beginning of the third, Berridge had said, 'There's no point trying to lie to you boys. Or lie to me, either. I've lost my nerve. Maybe I'm too old, or I've had too much time inside, I don't know. But I can feel inside my stomach I can't do it.' Parker and the others had known better than to try to get a man to do what he felt he was incapable of doing—they'd be too dependent on one another during the job—but it was too late by then to get somebody to take Berridge's place. This final Saturday night show before the Civic Auditorium was torn down was their only shot: a full house, all cash sales, no advance sales. Every dollar spent for a seat inside that jampacked soup bowl was still in this building, tonight only. So they'd altered the routine to go with a string of four instead of five, and the result was Briley in the guard's uniform, grinning, self-conscious to be in the trappings of Authority.

'How's it look?'

'It'll pass,' Parker said.

Keegan said, 'The pants are too short.'

Briley looked at him. 'You want me to send them out?'

'I only said.'

'You'll do,' Parker said.

'The hat was too big,' Briley said. 'I put some toilet paper around the brim.' He took the hat off, grinned at the inside, and put it back on. 'I'll go on out.'

Parker and Keegan waited half a minute, and then followed Briley out, Keegan carrying the toolkit again. They looked down to the right, and Briley was standing at the window, looking down at the musicians. There was no music right now, and the crowd noise was steadily dropping. Briley was standing in a good imitation of Dockery's original position; stomach jutting out, head forward and down, hands clasped behind his back.

Parker looked to his left, down through one of the windows at the platform in the middle of the auditorium. The four musicians who had been there were gone. Bulky stagehands in T-shirts and work pants, looking like citizens of a different planet from everybody else in the auditorium, were spreading a bright red carpet in the middle of the platform, moving the microphones and amplifiers around, and wheeling out a small keyboard instrument like a midget piano. In the middle of the red carpet was the white outline of a triangle, with an eye in it.

Keegan, beside Parker at the window, said, 'They shouldn't be able to get away with that.'

Parker frowned at the platform, not knowing what Keegan was talking about, but didn't ask.

Keegan said, 'That thing on the carpet there, that triangle. That's off the dollar bill. That's the kind of thing they do. Dress in the American flag, all that. None of them have any respect.'

Parker walked on to stand beside Briley, and Keegan followed. Briley, nodding at the platform, said, 'The headliners are coming.'

According to Morris, the final group would play a minimum of twenty-five minutes. If they were feeling good, if they'd established

an enjoyable rapport with the audience—
Morris had said, 'If the vibes are good'—they
might extend that to an hour or more. But
twenty-five minutes was the minimum, so
that was the deadline.

Parker looked at his watch: one
twenty-five. He said, 'We have to be out by
ten to two.'

Keegan said, 'Then we better move.'

'Let's wait for more noise.'

It was almost quiet out there now, the
crowd expectant and waiting. The stagehands
finished their adjustments and waddled off,
going back to the cigar butts they'd left on
table edges. The audience noise tapered off
even more, till individual coughs could be
heard, and suddenly the auditorium lights
went out, and they were looking down into
darkness.

Keegan was the only one who moved,
making an abrupt jump to the left, past the
edge of the window, the toolkit bumping his
knee and the wall. Parker and Briley
continued to stand there, side by side,
looking down; Briley in the guard uniform,
Parker in his dark jacket and the hood over
his face. The corridor lights above and behind
them remained on.

Keegan said, 'For Christ's sake, they can
see you!'

'A silhouette,' Parker said. 'With the light
behind me. Better they see a silhouette

standing still than jumping away and trying to hide.'

'I got out of the way before they could see me.'

The darkness wasn't total down there. A sparse pattern of dull red exit lights glowed. Tiny red and green dots of light from the platform showed that the amplifiers were working; those dots seemed to wink all at once, meaning that people were moving around on the platform.

The sound, when it came, had been anticipated for so long that it seemed unexpected, a surprise and a shock. An electronic crash, a chord of aggressive, whining, insistent notes blended into one detonation, an announcement of entry like the crash of an iron door back against an iron wall. An instant later one bright white beam flooded the platform from the ceiling, and there were now five musicians out there, one at the keyboard instrument, two with electric guitars, one at a complex array of drums, and one standing in the middle of the carpet's triangle, holding a hand microphone; this last one was dressed completely in red, and when the light came on he opened his mouth wide, held the microphone against his lower teeth, and shrieked loud enough to make distortions in the loudspeakers. The audience shrieked back, the four instrumentalists began a heavy background beat that was most like the sound of a highballing freight train—a sound out of context, since it was unlikely anyone in this audience had ever ridden a train of any kind—and the one in red began to sing/shout into the microphone: *'The-mes-sen-ger-of-Death-will-bring-you-down . . .'*

Parker said, 'It's time.'

He and Keegan turned away from the window. Parker counted doors and went to the one he wanted. He turned the knob and walked in, and the man at the desk dropped his pen and cried, 'Good God!'

'Take it easy,' Parker said. He took only one step into the room, then moved quickly to his left. Most of the left-hand wall was glass, and he didn't want to be seen by anyone on the other side of it, not yet. For the same reason, Keegan stayed in the doorway.

The man at the desk was about forty, very stocky in a soft-looking way. He wore horn-rim glasses, a dark gray suit, narrow tie, white shirt with button-down collar. He came from the same planet as the stagehands. He said, 'I don't have any money in here.' His voice was high-pitched and frightened; he might do something fatal simply out of nervousness.

Parker said, his voice as low and calm as possible with the competition of the music, 'We know that. We're not after you, we're not going to cause you any trouble.'

The man at the desk licked his lips, looking nervously at Keegan and then past Keegan toward the hall. 'What did you do with the ... what did you do with the man out there?'

'Mr. Dockery is perfectly all right. You'll be all right, too. There's nothing to worry about.'

Keegan came one step into the room, moved leftward to Parker's side, put the toolkit down, shut the door. The man at the desk began to look more frightened again.

Parker said, 'You'd be Mr. Stevenson, wouldn't you?'

'What? I—that's right. Who are you people?'

'Ronald Stevenson?'

'I haven't done anything to anybody. Why do you want—?'

'I told you we're not after you. What do your friends call you? Ron? Ronnie?'

'My—I'm, uh—Most people call me RG.'

'RG. Well, this is a robbery, RG. We're not here to hurt anybody or scare anybody. We're just going to take the money. The management is insured against this kind of thing, so, it's nothing for anybody to get killed over. We'd prefer a nice quiet operation, and so would you. So up to a point our interests are the same.'

'But I don't have any money.'

Keegan said, 'Next door they have money.'

Stevenson looked at the glass wall facing

38

his desk. The glass started at waist-height and continued up to within a foot of the ceiling. A three-foot width of ordinary wall was at this end, and a door with a glass panel in it was at the far end.

Parker said, 'Anybody looking at you, RG?'

'What?' Stevenson suddenly looked frightened again, and then guilty. 'No, not at all.'

'Look down at the paper on your desk, RG. Good. Pick up your pen. Start to write.'

Looking down at his desk top, Stevenson said, 'Write what?'

'Anything you want, RG. Just so the people next door see you looking normal.'

'Oh, I see.' Stevenson began to write. He didn't really look normal, his shoulders were too hunched, the position of his head too tense, but a casual glance from the next room wouldn't pick up that sort of detail.

Parker gave him half a minute to calm himself, and then said, 'Okay, RG, keep writing while I talk to you. There's three guards next door. What's the name of the one in charge?'

Still writing, looking down, Stevenson said, 'That would be Lieutenant Garrison.'

'First name?'

'I believe—It's Daniel, I believe.'

'Is he called Dan?'

Stevenson nodded at what he was writing.

39

'I've heard him called Dan, yes.' He was a precise man by nature, and now he was using that precision as a means of self-defense, as though to say, If I am very accurate and very proper, nothing bad will happen to me.

It was an idea Parker wanted to encourage. 'Good,' he said. 'And the other two? What names?'

Stevenson glanced up, looking through the glass into the other room again, as though to refresh his memory, then quickly looked back down at the paper, went on writing, and said, 'The younger one is Lavenstein, Edward Lavenstein. He's called Beau. And the other one is Hal Pressbury.'

'Dan Garrison, Beau Lavenstein, Hal Pressbury.'

'Yes, that's right.'

'Good. Keep writing, RG, this'll take a minute.'

Stevenson kept writing, though his shoulders hunched again. Parker touched Keegan's elbow, and Keegan nodded and went down on one knee beside the toolkit. Putting his automatic on the floor, he opened the toolkit and took out an automobile rear-view mirror; just the rectangular piece of silvered glass, without the metal housing or the mounting arm. Carrying the mirror, he traveled on all fours diagonally past Parker to the glass wall, staying under the bottom edge of the glass. When he got to the wall he

40

switched to a sitting position, legs crossed tailor-fashion and head stooped somewhat, and slowly raised the mirror up in front of him. He was sitting sideways to the wall, and had the mirror turned at an angle; when it was a little above his head, he said, 'Got'em.'

'What's it look like?'

'Double room. Double length, I mean.' The mirror moved slightly. 'Two doors to the hall, one near, one far. Sofa in between, one guard sitting at it. Table against the wall beyond the far door, one guard sitting in a chair at the table, facing the wall, playing solitaire.' The mirror moved. 'Four desks down the middle of the room, with adding machines. Three men, one woman. Cash on all four desks. They're counting it, banding it, dropping the stacks into metal trays on the floor. Back wall all filing cabinets, no door.' The mirror moved. 'Right wall, four windows. Table between windows two and three, with canvas sacks on it, most of them empty. Here comes the woman.' Silence for ten seconds; the mirror moved. 'The dough must have come upstairs in the sacks. She just took one of the full ones, carried it to the desk, emptied the bills out, put the empty sack back on the table. Now she's gone back to work.'

'Where's the third guard?'

'On the right.' The mirror moved. 'Leaning against the wall beside the money table. Kind of looking around at everything.'

'That'll be Garrison. RG, don't look up. Keep writing. Is Garrison the one beside the money?'

'He was, yes, the last I looked.'

'The young one, Beau Lavenstein, is he the one playing solitaire?'

'Yes, he was.'

Parker nodded. That made Hal Pressbury the one on the sofa. Parker said to Keegan, 'How many phones?'

The mirror moved. 'One, on the first desk.'

'RG, if you were going to call that number, what would you dial?'

'That's extension twenty-three.'

'Is that all you dial? Two three?'

'No. For an inside call, you dial nine first.'

'Nine two three, and that phone will ring?'

'That's right, yes.'

'Good. Now, RG, I want you to do me a favor. I want you to get up and go to the filing cabinet behind you. Open the top drawer and act as though you're looking for something. Good. Just like that. Stay there.'

Parker got down on hands and knees and crawled across the carpet and around behind the desk. Keegan kept watching the other room in the mirror, and Stevenson stood at the filing cabinet, his back to everything that was happening.

Parker raised himself cautiously behind the desk till he could look over the top. His first

42

sight of the room beyond showed him everything as Keegan had described it. No one was looking in this direction. The four clerks were working, Dan Garrison was looking at the money, Beau Lavenstein was looking at his card game, and Hal Pressbury was looking off into space and seemed to be mostly asleep.

Parker lifted his right arm and slid it across the desk top to the phone, then pulled the phone toward him. The cord ran off and down the side of the desk, so there was no problem about length. Parker took the phone off the desk top, put it on the floor, sat in front of it, and dialed 9 2 3. Faintly, through the glass and the distant sound of crowd-and-music in the auditorium, he heard the phone ring in the next room.

'It's a clerk,' Keegan said, and the receiver in Parker's hand clicked. A voice said, 'Hello?'

'A message for Edward Lavenstein,' Parker said.

'One moment, please.'

Parker waited. Keegan said, 'Here he comes. Garrison's watching, but he isn't moving.'

'Hello?'

'Beau?'

'Who's this?'

'Hold on a second, will you? There's a message.'

43

Parker lowered the phone and put his hand over the mouthpiece. Now, if there was trouble, no one from the next room would be using the phone; the line was tied up till Parker broke the connection at this end.

He said, 'RG, don't turn around. I've got more instructions for you. When I say to, you go over to the door, open it, and tell Garrison you want to see him. Get him to come in here. Stand to the left of the doorway when he comes in, so he doesn't see my partner. Talk to him as he's coming in, keep him distracted, say anything you want. When he's in, shut the door and say,"There are men pointing guns at you. I don't want anybody killed. I assured them we'd cooperate." You got that?'

'I think so.' Nervousness trembled in Stevenson's voice like a wind riffling curtains.

'Tell me what you're going to say after you shut the door.'

'There are men here with guns. I don't want anybody killed. I said we'd cooperate.'

'Fine. Go ahead now.'

Stevenson turned and walked toward the door. He moved unsteadily, as though he were very tired or a little drunk. Parker, keeping one hand folded over the mouthpiece of the phone, stretched out on his stomach behind the desk, so that his head and shoulders emerged past the desk's right side and he could see the door Stevenson was walking toward. His left hand, holding the phone receiver, was down at his side. His right hand was out in front of his face, resting the butt of the automatic on the carpet.

Stevenson reached the door, and grabbed for the knob as though he needed it to go on standing. He rested his other palm, shoulder-height, against the door frame, then opened the door and called, 'Lieutenant Garrison? Could you come here for a moment?'

Down by Parker's left hand, a tinny voice said, 'Hello? Hello?' A deeper echo sounded through the open door.

Keegan, his voice low, said, 'Here he comes. Easy as pie.'

Parker saw the feet first, saw Stevenson moving awkwardly to his left—the door opened to the right, making the move slightly cumbersome—heard Stevenson say, 'Well, there certainly is a lot of money tonight. A full house, eh? A fitting close for the old building. The new one just won't seem like home, will it? Here, let me—'

Garrison had seen neither Keegan nor Parker yet, and was standing in the doorway, waiting for Stevenson to tell him what he wanted. He was about Stevenson's age, forty-something, but was leaner and harder, with a deeply lined face. Stevenson was trying to reach behind him to shut the door.

Garrison moved reluctantly, saying, 'What

45

is it, Mr. Stevenson?' The voice was carefully neutral, but in its very neutrality, betrayed the contempt Garrison felt. So he was going to be another Dockery, and potentially more trouble.

Stevenson, in shutting the door, starting to lose his balance because of his nervousness, and had to cling to Garrison's right arm; that was perfect, and an unexpected bonus. Stevenson said, gasping suddenly, 'There are men with guns—Don't do anything, for the love of God!'

'What?' Garrison backed into the closed door, trying to push Stevenson away.

'Lieutenant Garrison, don't!'

Parker called, 'It's okay, Dan!'

Garrison, confused for a second by the sound of his own first name, stopped struggling with Stevenson and looked around, still seeing no more. 'What the hell is this?'

Parker had the automatic pointed at Garrison's chest. He called, 'RG, back up! Back up to your left.'

Stevenson hurriedly backed away, babbling as he went: 'I don't want anybody killed! I promised there'd be full cooperation! We're insured, it's all right, they're only after the money—'

Garrison came a quick step in from the door. His hand was near his holstered revolver, but not quite touching it. He saw Keegan suddenly, and tensed, frowning.

Parker said, 'Over here, Dan, here's where the gun is.' Garrison looked quickly toward the voice, and now he saw Parker and the gun. He made no move, but his expression got more grim.

Keegan, still watching through the mirror, said, 'They're getting interested.' Meaning one or more of the people in the other room had seen Stevenson's odd moves and were beginning to wonder.

Parker said, 'Dan, lie down on your face. Don't make me shoot your kneecap. I could set off a bomb in here tonight, nobody'd hear it anywhere outside. Get down.'

'You're not going to—'

'We don't have time, Dan. Down or I shoot, and I mean now.'

Stevenson, backed up against the front of the desk and leaning backward against it for support, cried, 'For God's sake, do it! It isn't worth getting killed over!'

'You'll pay,' Garrison said grimly, and got slowly down onto the floor.

Parker lifted the phone up to his ear again. 'Beau?'

'Who *is* this, dammit?'

Keegan said, 'The woman's talking to him. About the scene in here.'

Parker said, 'Beau, I want to tell you Dan Garrison is lying on his face in RG Stevenson's office, and two men have guns pointed at him. If you do anything hasty or stupid, they'll kill Dan and then rise up and kill you through the glass. You look at RG now, and he'll nod to tell you what I'm saying is true. Nod, RG.'

Parker looked up, and saw Stevenson's head lower and raise; a mechanical move, as though he were a newly completed robot trying the motion for the first time.

Keegan said, 'Hand over!'

'Get your hand off the mouthpiece, Beau! Don't wake Hal up, you'll just make trouble. Now turn your back to RG's office. Keep the phone up to your face, and put your other hand on top of your head. Leave it there.'

Keegan said, 'He's done it.'

Keeping an eye on Garrison, who was prone with his head arched up so he could see what was going on, Parker got his feet under him and stood. 'Move to the left, RG,' he said, and when Stevenson moved leftward, Parker had an unobstructed view of the room.

Everybody in there knew by now that something was wrong. Pressbury—a man about Dockery's age, but more gone to seed—was on his feet now and walking toward Lavenstein, a worried frown on his face. The three male clerks were all still at their desks, but none of them were working. All were looking at Lavenstein, who was facing them and not saying anything. The woman clerk—hers was the front desk, the one with the phone—was standing beside

48

Lavenstein, looking this way. Parker saw her see him and clutch at Lavenstein's side; in the earpiece of the phone he could faintly hear her saying something to Lavenstein and then Lavenstein's irritable voice, loud and clear, saying, 'I know, I know.'

To Keegan, Parker said, 'Take Dan.' Into the phone he said, 'Beau, tell Hal to stand where he is. Go on, tell him.'

'Stop there, Hal. They've got guns on us, stop there.'

'Tell him to put his hands on his head.'

'They say to put your hands on your head. Better do it, I guess.'

'Tell him to turn left.'

'They say turn left.'

'Tell him to back up until he's against the door.' Which would be the nearer door.

'They say you should back up against the door.'

'Tell the clerks to go over and sit on the sofa. The woman, too.'

'They want you people to go sit on the sofa.' The woman's voice yammered; her expression through the glass was outraged. 'You, too, Mrs. Kimberly. Yeah, but you better do it. They've got the upper hand now.'

Keegan said, 'He's de-fused.' He got to his feet with his own gun in his right hand and Garrison's revolver in his left. 'Only the one gun on him.'

The male clerks were all moving toward the sofa, the woman last and with the most reluctance. At the sofa, one of the male clerks suddenly bolted for the other door. The people around him all looked startled. He yanked the door open and dashed outside.

Keegan calmly opened the door between the rooms and headed down the window side of the room to cover everybody from the other end.

The clerk who'd made a dash for it backed into the room, hands over his head. In response to an order, he lowered one hand and shut the door. Keegan said something to him, and he sat down on the sofa. The others all joined him.

Parker said, 'RG, go next door and stand against the wall between Hal and the others.' He waited till Stevenson was in position, then said, 'Okay, Dan, you can get up now.'

Garrison got to his feet. He looked grim and angry. He stared at Parker and seemed to consider saying something, but just shook his head.

Parker said, 'Go next door, Dan, and stand to this side of Hal.'

Parker followed Garrison through and went over behind Lavenstein to take the revolver out of his holster and put it in his own hip pocket. Then he said, 'Hang up the phone, Beau. Go over and stand with your back to the door your friend ran out of.'

Keegan was down at the other end, back to the filing cabinets, automatic pointed in the general direction of the people along the side wall.

Parker walked over to Hal Pressbury, who was looking cranky and crotchety, and who said, 'You people can't get away with this sort of thing. You think this is the Wild West?'

'Turn around, Hal.'

'So you can shoot me in the back? You'll have to look me in the eye, you son of a bitch.'

'Hal, you either turn around so I can disarm you, or I'll have to knock you out.'

'I'll meet you face to face.'

Parker put the automatic in his left hand, raised his right fist in front of his shoulder, and punched Pressbury between the eyes. Pressbury's head snapped back, bouncing off the door, and his face went slack. With a hand to his chest, Parker kept him from falling forward and let him slide down the door to a sitting position. Then he took Pressbury's revolver, patted him briefly to be sure he had no other weapons, and backed away from him.

Garrison said tightly, 'That's something else you'll pay for.'

'We may pay later,' Parker said, turning his head back and forth so they'd know he was talking to all of them, 'but any one of you people who disobeys us will pay now.' He walked over to the sofa, keeping the automatic in his left hand, and stood in front of the clerk who'd tried ducking out the door. 'Stand up,' he said.

The clerk was afraid now. 'What do you want from me?'

'You've disobeyed once. Don't make it twice. Stand up.'

The woman, sitting beside him, said, 'You'd better do what he says, George.'

George, blinking, trying to fit an expression of bravado onto his face, leaned forward to get up and Parker hit him on the nose. George bounced back into the sofa, and Parker waited to see if his nose would start bleeding. The woman said something shocked and angry, everybody stirred, and George put his hand to his face. When he took it away to look at it, his fingertips were red; a drop of blood hit his shirt.

The woman said, 'Oh, you're bleeding!' and started busily to reach into her sleeve.

Parker said, 'Nobody touches him. He doesn't use a handkerchief or a tissue or any cloth. George? You can put your head back, but keep your hands away from your face.'

The woman said, 'You people are inhuman!'

'Then you should be very cautious with us,' Parker said. He turned his back on them all and went over to the nearest desk, where he put down the automatic and took the two

52

guards' guns from his hip pockets. Behind him, he knew they were all watching George, who was in a position none of them would want to be in for himself; not dangerous, but uncomfortable and humiliating. Head back, blood dribbling from his nose, having to gulp and gasp when he breathed. Nobody else would want to wind up like that, so the others would be less likely now to try something stupid.

Keegan kept them all covered. Originally, of course, Berridge would have been the man outside, and Keegan and Briley would both have watched the prisoners, one at either end of the room. There was more menace implicit in being unable to look at all the guns facing you at the same time. But Parker had been making up for that in other ways.

Now he took the blue laundry bag from his pocket, ripped open the outer plastic—it was the toughest thing to do so far, with the work gloves on—and then shook open the bag. He swept all the loose unbanded bills from the desk into the bag, and next emptied the banded stacks of bills from the trays beside the desk. The second desk filled the bag, and he took a rubber band from his side trouser pocket and closed the neck of the bag. Then he carried the bag, which was pretty heavy now, into Stevenson's office and left it beside the hall door. He picked up the toolkit, carried it into the room, and put it on the first desk, beside the phone. This one was hung up, but the one on Stevenson's desk was still off the hook, so a call to either of these numbers would produce a busy signal.

Keegan had the second blue bag. He tossed it to Parker, who opened it and filled it with the bills at the third and fourth desks.

Now there was a minor error in the routine, the result of the last-minute change from Berridge. Briley had the third laundry bag, and was in the hall; when they'd made the switch of assignments, nobody'd thought to change that one detail. Which was why normally Parker preferred to let a job go rather than make late changes in the pattern. This time the problems hadn't seemed very large, and the job itself was tempting, so he'd relaxed a rule for himself. With any luck, this business with the laundry bag was the only place a seam would show.

Parker closed the top of the second bag with another rubber band and carried it in to put it beside the first. Then he opened the hall door, and Briley spun at once and showed him Dockery's revolver; then he grinned and put the revolver away again.

The music noise was louder out here. Parker called, 'The laundry bag.'

'By God, you're right. It's in my jacket, in the john.'

'Get it. There's room for your clothes in it.'

'Good,' Briley said, and hurried off toward

the men's room.

Parker stayed in the doorway, watching both ways. This was where a small seam could become a big tear that would rip the whole job open. If someone came up here while Briley was around, Briley could act officious and send him on his way. If someone came up now, it would be a complication. They were dependent on luck, for good or ill, and that was no way to set things up.

Should he have let it go with just the two bags' worth? They had the money from all the desks, but not the unsorted money in the canvas bags still on the table. To leave that behind would be a failure in a different direction; the job had a seam in it, that was all.

Briley came back with the third bag, open and already with contents. It had been planned all along to include the substitute guard's clothing in one of the bags with the money, if there was room. If not, the guard would either have made a quick change on the roof, having carried his own clothing that far, or waited till they were back in the theater.

Briley handed over the bag and said, 'You should have seen that boy when he came out the door and I throwed down on him. I wish I'd had a camera.'

'We'll be out in five minutes,' Parker said.

'Take your time. I'm getting so I like this music.'

Parker shut the door and went back to finish stacking the money. The third bag wasn't quite as full as the other two, even with Briley's clothes in the bottom. Parker put it with the others, went back to the main room, and said, 'You people on the sofa, get up.' Pressbury was standing again now, and looking mulish but not dangerous. Parker said, to the four clerks, 'Turn around and face the sofa. Beau, come over and stand at the end of the line. Hal, come up to the other end. RG, stand beside Hal. Dan, you stand beside RG.'

The eight people stood in a row, facing the wall. Parker took the sets of handcuffs from the toolkit, started with Garrison, and handcuffed them all together, finished with Beau Lavenstein at the other end, and had one set of cuffs left. He said, 'Everybody turn right. We're going into the corner over there.'

It was the far corner of the exterior wall, between the windows and the filing cabinets. One of the marks of this building's age was the heat pipes that ran up beside the walls in the corners of all the rooms. Parker now arranged the eight people so that Lavenstein was just to the left of this pipe, facing the filing cabinet, the others made a circle, all facing outward, and Garrison, the other end of the line, was just to the right of the pipe, facing toward the windows. Parker cuffed

56

Garrison's and Lavenstein's free hands together, with the cuff chain running behind the pipe. Now they were all limited to the corner of the room, where they couldn't reach the phone or a door or a window, and were in a circle facing outward so that even communication with one another would be difficult.

Parker and Keegan put all the guns in the toolkit, and Keegan carried it when they went into Stevenson's office. Parker left Stevenson's phone off the hook—it was still better for a caller to get a busy signal than no answer—and opened the door to put all three laundry bags outside. Keegan went out, carrying the toolkit, and Parker followed him and shut the door. Now Parker carried two of the laundry bags, and Keegan one laundry bag and the toolkit, and they followed Briley down the hall and up the stairwell, Briley checking things out at every stage of the trip.

It went without trouble. The music still pounded away down there, the audience was even louder than before, and it was likely the show would run over the minimum length. Still it was not quite ten minutes to two, their deadline, and they were well on their way.

The upstairs office was as they'd left it. Briley ran up the furniture staircase, and Keegan and Parker handed up the three laundry bags and two toolkits. They'd turned the light on when entering the room, and

Parker turned it out again after Keegan and Briley were both out and up on the roof. Then he followed them.

Morris had come over from the fire escape. 'Not a bit of trouble,' he said.

'Nor us,' Briley said.

'Here's something,' Keegan said. He was still finding things to be disgusted about. 'That lousy Berridge has us loused up. We've got five things to carry and now there's only four of us.'

Morris said, 'I'll carry two. I've had a nice long rest. I'll carry the money.'

Morris went first, carrying two of the laundry bags. Briley followed, with the bag containing his own clothes, followed by Keegan and Parker, each with a toolkit, Parker carrying the kit that had been left upstairs, the one with the snaps on the outside for carrying the ax.

It was strange not to hear the music. Going down the fire escape, they heard the sounds of the city instead; few sounds at this hour, mostly traffic.

The Strand Theater's fire door looked the same as usual, but was different in that it had been unlocked from the inside. Grasping the lip overhang at the bottom, it was possible to pull the door open.

Keegan had the flashlight, and didn't turn it on until they were all in the theater and Parker had closed and relocked the door.

58

Then the light shone out across the cluttered empty stage—this had been a vaudeville theater long ago, when it was first built and movies weren't important yet—and they picked their way slowly through the rubble; the screen, sound system, and some other things had already been stripped out of this building.

The third toolkit and the *Union Electric Co.* coveralls were where they'd left them, in seats near the back of the theater. Briley scaled the guard's hat through the darkness toward the stage, and they all took off their masks and put on the coveralls. Keegan had put the flashlight on an armrest at the end of an aisle, pointing its light toward the stage, and their movements in front of it as they put on the coveralls made bat-shadows fly all over the high empty interior of the building.

Morris went first, carrying a toolkit out to the truck, waiting for them in front of the marquee. They heard him start the truck engine, and then the rest of them came out, carrying things, Parker and Keegan making two trips. The street was almost deserted, only two cars going by in the time it took them to load the truck. Parker sat up front beside Morris, Keegan and Briley sat in back on the bags of money, and Morris drove them away from there.

The first time they were stopped at a traffic light, Morris said, 'Any trouble in there?'

'No. It went the way it was supposed to.' He thought about the laundry bag in the wrong place, and being short one man to carry things away from there, but they were points too minor to mention.

'Sounded like nice music.'

Parker had nothing to say to that. The light turned green, and they drove on.

The house they were heading for, Keegan had rented two weeks ago, though none of them had been there since, until they'd left their cars in the neighborhood and suitcases in the house earlier today. It had taken Keegan four full days to find a house that suited their needs, and this one had checked out right down the list. In the first place, it was owned by a realty corporation rather than an individual, which meant that so long as the rent was paid, no one would be dropping by to chat with the tenant. Second, its neighbors on both sides were commercial concerns that closed in the evening—a supermarket on one side, a hobby shop on the other. It had a garage and a good-sized backyard, all enclosed by a high board fence. It had come furnished, including a phone, so no one would be wondering why the house was standing empty, particularly since Keegan, the day he took the place, had set time switches that turned lamps on at six P.M. every day in the living room and one of the upstairs bedrooms, and switched them off again a little past midnight.

It was called Dornwell Street, and the house number was 426. When Morris drove the *Union Electric Co.* truck down Dornwell Street now, it was silent and dark and empty, the buildings black on both sides, the only illumination coming from wide-spaced streetlights. Morris turned into the driveway at 426, cut the headlights, and came to a stop. Keegan climbed out of the back of the truck and trotted up to open the garage door, a segmented aluminum door that slid upward. Morris drove the truck into the garage, and then all four of them carried everything into the house, turning on a small worklight over the stove in the kitchen, until they had themselves and everything else inside. Then they switched on the round fluorescent light in the middle of the ceiling.

Keegan had stocked the place with food this morning, and now he and Morris stayed in the kitchen to broil some steaks while Briley and Parker carried the blue plastic laundry bags into the dining room.

The dining room had no windows, and the wide entryway to the living room could be closed by sliding doors recessed into the walls. They closed these doors now, and then switched on the overhead light fixture and emptied the first of the laundry bags onto the dining-room table. They'd chosen the bag with Briley's clothes in it first, and Briley

61

went away to change while Parker sat at the table and began the split.

They would stay here two or three days, depending on what the radio told them about the local law activity. The cars they had parked around the neighborhood were all clean, and shouldn't attract any attention.

Briley came to the side doorway, which they'd left open because it didn't expose them to any windows. He said, 'Parker.'

'What is it?'

'You better come take a look.'

Parker got up from the table and went with him. The hall led to the front door at one end and the kitchen at the other, with the living and dining rooms opening off it along the way. The staircase was across the hall from the living room, with the bathroom between it and the kitchen. Briley, still in his coveralls, his clothes still over his arm, led the way to the bathroom and stood aside for Parker to go in. He'd already turned the light on.

Berridge was lying on his back on the floor. The side of his head had been punched in, and a plumber's wrench with the end bloody and hair-matted was lying on the floor between the body and the toilet.

They searched the house and it was empty.

PART TWO

CHAPTER ONE

Parker turned in at the new mailbox, with the name *Willis* on it. That was the name Claire was using here, because at one time Parker had lived under the name Charles Willis, and Claire was trying to make her presence in his life retroactive to the time before they'd met. So she was going to be Claire Willis for a while.

At the hotel in New York, where she was either to have been waiting for him or to have left a message, there'd been a message. He'd known when he'd taken the sealed envelope from the desk clerk that it meant she'd found a house. Somewhere in the northeast.

It turned out to be here, seventy miles from New York, tucked away in a rural corner where the state lines of New York and New Jersey and Pennsylvania all meet. It was a small house, country-looking, part gray stone and part brown shingling, built in the middle of a deep rectangular tree-covered lot between this blacktop road and the edge of a lake called Colliver's Pond. The driveway was crushed stone, there were trees and underbrush all around the house instead of lawn, and the two-car attached garage looked almost as big as the rest of the place. The end garage doors were open, old-fashioned doors that swung out to both sides, showing an empty space inside. Next to it, in the half-light, stood Claire's blue Buick, a legal car bought under her own name. The Pontiac Parker was driving was a mace, bought outside the law but with papers good enough to pass a normal inspection; a car on nobody's wanted list.

Parker drove the Pontiac into the garage, took the two suitcases out of the trunk, put them out on the crushed-stone driveway, and was closing the garage doors when Claire came out of the main entrance of the house, wearing slacks and a white sweater, with a cloth tied around her head. She smiled but didn't say anything, and came walking toward him as he finished closing the doors. She was tall and slender and self-possessed, with the face and figure of a fashion model, and as she reached him she put a very remote expression on her face, through which the smile still shone, and said, 'Mr Lynch?'

That was the name he'd had the first time they'd met. She needed to keep touching things, to be sure they were still there, and when what she touched was the past, Parker had nothing to say back to her. His past didn't exist. He said, 'Hello.' At the same time he didn't want to rebuff her, so he reached his arms out and drew her in close.

She nuzzled his throat and said, 'You smell like money.'

He laughed, a barking sound. 'That's the suitcase. I'll show it to you.'

'And I'll show you the house.' She stepped away from him, but kept one of his hands. 'What do you think of it, so far?'

He didn't think about houses, they had as much to do with his life as apple trees. But she needed an answer, so he said, 'It looks fine. The outside.'

'There's all sorts of advantages for us,' she said. 'Come on in, I'll tell you about it.'

Parker had to take his hand back to carry one of the suitcases. She went on ahead to open the door, and he carried the two bags. At the entrance, he nodded to the right and said, 'Neighbors are close.' Spring foliage was skimpy on the trees, and a white clapboard house could be seen less than fifty feet away on that side.

'That's one of the nice things,' she said. 'Come on in, I'll tell you everything.' Holding the door, she said, 'You hungry?'

'Later. After I shower.'

It was a large country kitchen he'd entered, with old electrical appliances around the walls, an old porcelain double sink under the windows facing the neighbor's house, and a red-and-yellow-patterned linoleum on the floor so old the lines of the floorboard underneath could be seen clearly through it. The formica-and-chrome kitchen set in the middle of the room was twenty years newer

67

than everything else, but still thirty years old.

Claire shut the door. 'We don't have any neighbors. Both sides, empty almost all year. Come here, let me show you.'

Parker had put the suitcases down against the wall. Now he followed Claire through a wide doorway at the far left corner of the kitchen and into a large living room. Where the two garages took the front left quarter of the house and the kitchen most of the front right quarter, this living room filled the left rear quarter, behind the garages. In the middle of the wall it shared with the garage space was a stony fireplace. Directly opposite the fireplace was a door, with several small-paned windows stretching away on both sides. Through these windows, and the glass in the door, the lake could be seen, and a small structure of some kind down by the water's edge.

Claire led the way diagonally across the living room—it was furnished in maple tables and mohair chairs, all old and battered and lodge-looking—and through the door to a screened porch overlooking the lake. The air was cooler on this side of the house. She said, 'It's a lake. Most of the houses are just for the summer. The real estate woman told me there's only fifteen-percent occupancy around the lake year round, and most of that is across there on the other side, because this side gets the wind in the wintertime. So we can live here all year without any neighbors, and then go somewhere else in the summer. That's normal, too, a lot of people rent their houses in the summer. We can do the same.'

She was proud of herself, and it sounded in her voice. Parker knew she'd done her house searching with his specific needs at the top of her list, and she'd found a place that was perfect, and she was pleased with herself. He said, 'It must have been hard to find a place like this.'

She smiled. 'It took a while. But you can relax here, you don't have to be on guard.'

There was no answer to that. He was on guard everywhere, it was natural to him. He said, 'What's that building down by the water?'

'A boathouse. There's no boat, though. Want to see it?'

There was a slate walk from the porch steps across to the boathouse. Stumps showed where trees had been sawed away to give a clearer view of the lake from the house, but there were still several trees standing, and underbrush between. Boulders lined the water's edge, with ropy shrubs growing out over some of them, and a wooden dock ran out over the water along the side of the boathouse.

There were spider webs across the closed boathouse door. Claire brushed them away, saying, 'They build these new every day. I

69

wish they'd get discouraged.' She opened the door, pushing it inward, and stepped inside, saying, 'The floor's very narrow here.'

The boathouse was about twelve feet wide and twenty-five feet long, with a concrete floor about eighteen inches wide along three sides. A vertical garage door closed the wide opening in the fourth wall; through its grimy windows the far shore of the lake could be seen. Water lapped at the concrete inside the boathouse about two feet below floor-level.

Claire said, 'We can get a boat, if you want.'

Parker never liked to be in a place with only one exit, boat or boathouse included. He said, 'Maybe later on. Let me get used to a house first.'

Her smile was a bit crooked. 'That will be different, won't it?'

They went back to the house. Parker had met Claire three years before, in Indianapolis. She was an airline pilot's widow, and an in-law of her dead husband, a coin dealer named Billy Lebatard, had involved her in a coin convention robbery. Lebatard was an amateur with a rich fantasy life, and at the end the job went very sour, Lebatard was killed, there was bloodshed everywhere, and Parker had dragged Claire out of the way at the last minute. They'd been together since then, but her one experience of his profession had been enough, particularly after the

70

husband she'd lost in an airplane. Now she wanted to know none of the details of the ventures he went on, not even where he was going or how long he expected to be gone. When he was around they lived together—in resort hotels, mostly, up till now—and when he was gone she waited for him.

In the living room again, she said, 'I've been expecting you to show up at night, so I've been making a fire after dinner. I wanted to have a fire going when you came in.'

'We'll make one a little later.'

'It doesn't matter what time of day you get here,' she said.

They went back to the kitchen and he put one of the suitcases up on the kitchen table. She sat in one of the chrome tube chairs and watched. The suitcase was closed with two belts and three snaps; Parker opened the belts, used a key to unlock and open the snaps, and then lifted the lid. He took out the two sweaters on top, dropped them on a chair, and the suitcase was full of bills.

Claire grinned at the money. 'I must say it looks good.'

'There's twelve thousand. I took away seventeen but I stashed five.' He had several caches around the country, for emergencies. Back when the Charles Willis name had been blown, back from before he'd met Claire, all his original caches had been lost to him. He was still, four years later, rebuilding them.

71

'Can I spend some of it on the house?'

'You can spend it any way you want.'

'I want to get some better furniture. And a decent kitchen.'

'Do we have a basement?'

'Just under part of the house. You get into it through the garage.'

'We'll want to have a place to stow some of this.'

'I started a checking account in town. It's about six miles back toward New York.'

'We can't go there with twelve grand in a suitcase.'

She laughed, shaking her head. 'No, I thought I'd deposit two or three hundred a week, whatever we need. There's something solid and dependable about a checking account. I want this house to have such a perfectly legal and normal look to it that nobody will ever even think twice about it.'

'For me?'

She looked sharply at him, then smiled and said, 'All right. For both of us. But partly for you.'

'I appreciate it.'

'And if I have a nesting instinct, that's part of what makes me a woman.'

'I didn't argue.'

She looked around the room, looked at him again, shook her head. 'You make me feel like I'm trying to domesticate a gorilla.'

He closed the lid down over the money.

'Gorillas have mates.'

'You aren't a gorilla,' she said. 'And I'm not trying to domesticate you. It's just strange to have you here, that's all.'

Parker looked at her. Most of the time he didn't think about it, but every once in a while he realized she was important to him. He made his voice and his face softer, and said, 'We'll both get used to it.'

'I know we will.'

'I'll take the shower now.'

The final quarter of the house, behind the kitchen and beside the living room, contained the bedroom and adjoining bath. Both rooms had windows overlooking the lake, and a door led from the bedroom out onto the same broad porch he'd been to before from the living room. Both rooms were connected to the kitchen, and had a connecting door between them as well. The bathroom, being in the corner, had windows in two walls, both glazed.

These rooms, too, were old-fashioned, with a brass double bed and tall wooden chifforobe in the bedroom and a lion-foot tub with a plastic shower curtain hanging from a rod over it in the bathroom. Parker put both suitcases away in the bedroom closet, stripped, and took a hot shower, standing on a rubber mat in the white tub. While he was still there, the shower curtain opened and

Claire stuck her head in. 'Is there room for two?'

'Plenty.' He put his hand out to help her, and she stepped over the side of the tub and in.

'Steamy.' She turned in a circle, getting completely wet. Then he kissed her, sliding his hand down the long slick line of her back, the hot water streaming down their faces, and she raised her dripping arms lazily to close them around his neck.

CHAPTER TWO

Parker sat looking into the fire. A night wind had come up, and wood made small creaking noises in the top of the house. There was a low attic up there, he'd looked it over earlier today, and it was as full of noises now as a ship at anchor.

Claire had turned off all the lights in the living room, so their only sources of illumination were the fire and light-spill from the kitchen. It made Parker nervous, the semi-darkness and the anonymous sounds, but he understood there was nothing to beware of here, and he knew the atmosphere would make Claire happy, so he said nothing.

She was sitting beside him on the sofa, leaning her shoulder against his, and after a long silence she said, 'What are you thinking about?'

'I have to call Handy McKay.' Handy, who used to be in the same profession and was retired to his own diner now in Presque Isle, Maine, was Parker's contact with the rest of the bent world. Anybody who wanted to get in touch with Parker about a job or anything along those lines had to call Handy, who would pass on the message.

'Don't call him tonight.'

'I don't intend to.'

'In the morning.'

He didn't say anything.

She said, 'Is this going to be too dull for you?'

'I like it.'

'You're sure?' Doubt and fear were evident in her voice.

'If we want a vacation somewhere else,' he said, 'we can go, and then come back.'

'That's right.' She sounded happier.

'For now I like it.' He tried to find a way to let her know he was telling the truth, and finally said, 'I can feel my shoulders getting loose.'

'That's good,' she said, and leaned closer to him. He could smell her perfume and the fire, intermixed.

A little later she said, 'Would you tell me about where you were?'

'You mean the job?'

'Yes.'

'You said you never wanted to hear about it.'

'I feel different now. I still don't think I want to know anything ahead of time. But when it's over, and you're back, I think I'd like to hear. Unless you don't want to tell me.'

'I don't mind.'

She abruptly sat up and leaned forward to pick up her cigarettes from the coffee table. Keeping her face turned away, so that she was a silhouette between him and the fire, she said, 'Sometimes I wish I was attracted to normal average everyday men who live quiet safe lives and never make anybody nervous.'

This had been between them since the beginning. She was only interested in men whose lives were dangerous, but when she had one she wished he'd be more careful. Parker said, 'I know. Your husband. And the stock-car racer.'

'And you.'

'I'm the worst of all.'

'I moved into this house over a week ago. Every night I sat here like this, and I couldn't even anticipate. I picked the house with you in mind, and I didn't know if you'd ever see it.'

'I know.'

'You *are* the worst of all, dammit. With the others, at least I knew where they were, I knew what they were facing, and if something

76

happened I knew about it right away. But you, some day you'll go off and you never will come back and how will I know when to stop waiting?'

This came over her from time to time, and there was never anything Parker could say to her. He wouldn't lie to her, and he had no reassuring truths to say. He intended to go on being careful, within his own definition of the word, but it was true that something could always happen, that it might be one time that he wouldn't get back. Once he'd tried to point out to her that it was no good spoiling the times he *did* come back by worrying about his not returning sometime in the future, but she'd thought that kind of attitude was unfeeling, so he hadn't mentioned it any more. Now all he did was wait it out.

She sat hunched forward a minute longer, smoking, looking angrily at the surface of the coffee table. Then she shook her head and threw the cigarette into the fire and turned her head to say, 'I'm sorry. I have to open the valve every once in a while, I guess, and let some of the steam out. Will you tell me about this last time? What kind of place was it? Not another coin convention.'

'No. A rock-and-roll concert.'

She grinned uncertainly. 'You're kidding.'

'No.' He went on to tell her the whole story, from beginning to end. He left out only two things: the names of the people he was with, because they wouldn't mean anything to her, and the discovery of Berridge's dead body in the house afterward. None of them had been able to figure out what Berridge was doing there—he'd known about the place, of course, from the earlier meetings, but there'd been no reason for him to go there the night of the job—nor had they turned up the guy who'd killed him. They'd stayed in the house three days, having removed Berridge to the basement that first night, and the killer hadn't come back. Keegan had been full of explanations, but none of them had sounded probable, and in the end none of them had mattered, because they'd split the take and waited out the manhunt and left the house to go their separate ways, and the death of Berridge had affected them not at all. Parker left the death out for two reasons: because he knew it would disturb her, and because it raised unanswerable questions that didn't matter but that he knew would plague her mind.

At the end, when he was finished describing the routine to her, she said, 'So it went just right, didn't it?'

'Mostly.'

'If only they could all be like that. Simple, safe and finished with, and back you come.'

'That's right,' he said.

CHAPTER THREE

The fourth day he was at the house, he was working on a stash hole in the basement when Claire called down the stairs, 'Handy McKay on the phone.'

He went upstairs, and she was waiting for him. 'We don't need money yet,' she said. 'Let's see what he's got.'

Parker went into the living room and picked up the phone. He identified himself, and Handy's voice said, 'Did your friend Keegan get in touch with you?' He sounded vaguely worried.

'No. Should he?'

'He called last night, said he had to talk to you about that time you were together last week. Said it was important, but he couldn't say much.' Nor could Handy, not on the phone.

Parker said, 'Why should *he* call me? Why not you?'

'He said he was moving around, didn't have a place he could be reached. It was definitely Keegan, from things he said. And moving around, not having a place he could be reached, I figured maybe that meant he really *should* get in touch with you.' Meaning that to Handy it had sounded as though Keegan might be having trouble with the law, which naturally Parker would have to be told about.

Parker said, 'So you told him where I was?' That wasn't the way it was supposed to work. Handy passed messages on to Parker, didn't give Parker's whereabouts to other people.

Particularly not now, not Claire's house.

Sounding more worried, Handy said, 'Your phone number. It really sounded strong. I had to make a decision.'

'I suppose. All right.'

'But today I thought it over, and I figured I'd better call you and make sure.'

'Okay. I'll handle it.'

'I hope I didn't louse you up.'

'Me, too.'

Parker hung up and went to the kitchen, where Claire was sitting reading a magazine with her lunch. He said, 'Handy gave out this number.'

She looked at him. 'What does that mean?'

'I don't know yet. He gave it to one of the people I was on that last job with.'

'When did he give it to him?'

'Last night.'

She closed the magazine. 'And he hasn't called, so that means something's wrong.'

'Yes.'

'What?'

'I don't know yet.'

'What do we do about it?'

'You go to New York. Move into a hotel

80

for a few days.'

'Move?'

'Just until I go talk to Keegan. That's his name.'

'I don't want to leave my house,' she said.

'We don't know what Keegan wanted it for. Or who he wanted it for. I can't leave you alone here.'

She got to her feet, frowning, looking angry and irritable. 'I'm not going to go away from my house. I just got this house, I'm not going away from it.' She went over to the sink with her plate and cup, turned the water on, left it on and stood there with her back to him.

Parker walked around the table and stood beside her. 'I can't wait here for it, not knowing what it is. I have to go see Keegan. I know where he was headed from the job, I'll go there and see him and find out what's going on. But what if there's trouble from somebody else, and they come here while I'm gone?'

'Leave me a gun.'

'That isn't sensible.'

Both hands gripping tight to the lip of the sink, as though she was prepared to resist being dragged physically out of the house, she turned her head and stared coldly at him and said, 'I am not going to leave my house.'

He hesitated, then shrugged and turned away. 'I'll be back as soon as I can.'

CHAPTER FOUR

Keegan was nailed to the wall. His naked body had been cigarette-burned and scratched with a knife-tip, but it was probably the bleeding around the nails in his forearms that had killed him. He looked shriveled and small hanging there, his feet crumpled against the floor beneath him.

Keegan was a drinker who liked isolation, so there'd been no need to gag him. This Minnesota farmhouse surrounded by dairy grazing land was half a mile from the nearest neighbor. He could be left to either scream or tell the people torturing him what they wanted to know.

Parker touched the corpse's chest, and it was cold; they must have started on him very soon after he'd made his call to Handy. Had they been with him then—was it for them he'd phoned Handy?

It was now shortly after midnight. Parker had driven from Claire's house to Newark Airport, had taken the first plane to Minneapolis, and had stolen a white Dodge station wagon in the airport parking lot for the forty-five-mile drive to this house. He'd seen the house for the last quarter mile or more, all lit up as though for a night wedding, but when he'd gotten here the light had shone on empty rooms and silence. He'd entered the house cautiously, searched it room by room, and at last he'd found Keegan nailed to an upstairs bedroom wall, long since dead.

And the house torn apart. Besides what they'd done to Keegan, they'd ripped the house open from top to bottom, looking for something. The fact that no rooms at all were left unstripped suggested they hadn't found what they were looking for.

In the kitchen, there'd been dishes in the sink and on the table to show where two men had eaten two meals, a dinner and a breakfast. So they'd been out of here already by the time Handy had called Parker today at noon.

Parker made a fast surface scan of the house, and then left. He'd worn rubber gloves inside, except when he'd stripped one off so he could feel the coldness of Keegan's chest, and now he stood beside the Dodge and peeled the gloves off, put them in his pocket, and held his hands out in the air a minute, flexing the fingers, letting the skin get dry and cool. He frowned toward the house, thinking. Berridge dead; Keegan tortured and dead, his house searched. Keegan trying to locate Parker, just before the torturing started. Somebody wanted something, and the connecting link was Berridge.

Why kill Berridge back in the hideout?

After killing him, why not stick around?

Because four men would be showing up, and these were only two. Better to wait till the four split up, and go after them one at a time. Follow one home, start with him, locate the others through him.

All three others? Or just Parker? And how were they traveling? Could they be on the East Coast already?

Parker got into the Dodge and headed back toward Minneapolis. After fifteen miles he saw the light of a phone booth outside a closed gas station in a silent empty dark town. The phone booth, three streetlights, a yellow blinker at the only intersection, that was the extent of the illumination in the town. Parker rolled to a stop beside the phone booth, cut the Dodge's lights, left the motor running, and got out. He had a pocket full of change, which he took out while walking to the phone booth and put on the metal tray in there. He left the door open, so the interior light stayed off, only the light on top continuing to shine. When the blinker signal at the intersection was on, there was enough light to dial by; when it was off, he paused for a second with his finger waiting in front of the dial.

An operator came on to tell him how much, and he put the coins in during the phases of yellow light. Then there was a long silence punctuated by clicks, one ring sound, and Claire's voice: 'Hello?'

'It's me. How are things?'

'Fine. How are you?'

'No visitors?'

'Nobody at all. Will you be back soon?'

'My friend died of a lingering illness. Very painful illness.'

A little silence, and then a small voice: 'Oh.'

Only so much could be said on a telephone. 'You ought to take a day or two off. Go to New York, do some shopping.'

'I don't want to leave my house,' she said.

'This is serious!'

'So am I. Tomorrow I'll buy a dog.'

'I'm talking about tonight.'

'I'll be all right. I went out and got a rifle.'

Parker frowned at the phone. He wanted to tell her a house with all those windows, all those exterior doors, couldn't be defended, not with a rifle, not with a dog. Not against two men who nail a man to a wall and burn him with cigarettes. But you couldn't say things to a telephone that you wouldn't be willing to say to a district attorney, so he tried to get his meaning into his voice instead of his words: 'I think you ought to go away.'

'I know what you think,' she said, and then tried to soften it, saying, 'I know you're worried about me. But you just don't know what this house means to me. I *can't* go away from it, not after I just got into it. I won't be *driven* away from it.'

85

There was a little silence then while he thought, until she said, 'Hello? Are you there?'

'I'm here.'

He was thinking about going back, waiting for them to show up. His instinct was against it; when the opposition is coming at you, the best place to be is on their back trail, coming up behind them. But how could he leave Claire in the house alone?

The decision was hers. He had to handle it the way he knew was right, no matter what. He said, 'What you do right now, you pack everything there that's mine and get it out. Stow it all in one of the empty houses around there. But do it now, don't wait till morning.'

'You don't have that much here.'

'So it won't take long. If anybody comes looking for me, you don't fight them. Understand me? You don't fight them.'

'What do I do instead?'

'Tell them you just run a message service, you only see me two or three times a year, when I give you some money for taking care of my messages. What you tell them, any time a message comes for me you call the Wilmington Hotel in New York and leave it for me in the name of Edward Latham. You got that?'

'Yes. But what—?'

'Give me the names back.'

'Is it important?'

'Yes. Those are the names to use.'

'Wilmington Hotel. Edward—I'm sorry.'

'Latham. Edward Latham.'

She repeated the name. 'Is that all?'

'Don't antagonize them. They're very mean people.'

'I know how to be a little mouse,' she said.

'That's good. I'll get back there as soon as I can.'

'I know you will.'

'Clean my stuff out of there right away.'

'I will.'

He broke the connection, put in a dime, dialed 2125551212, got the Wilmington Hotel's phone number from New York City Information, dialed it, pumped more change in the box, and got the desk clerk.

'I want to make a reservation for three days starting Thursday.'

'Name, sir?'

'Latham. Edward Latham.'

'Home address?'

'Newcastle Business Machines, Minneapolis, Minnesota.'

'That's a single, sir?'

'Yes.'

'For three nights.'

'Yes.'

'We will hold the reservation until three P.M. on Thursday.'

'Yes, I know.'

'Thank you for calling the Wilmington, sir.'

Parker broke the connection again and dialed a number in Chicago. It rang six times, and then a heavy male voice came on, saying, 'I hope to hell this isn't a wrong number. You know what time it is?'

'I'm looking for a fellow named Briley. He and I just did some musical work together.'

'You the guy called the day before yesterday?'

'No. That was Keegan.'

'He called at a better time of day, my friend, but I'll tell you just what I told him. Our friend is partying in Detroit. No fixed abode.'

'No contact? You're supposed to be his contact.' As Handy was Parker's.

'I know what I'm supposed to be. You know a girl in Detroit named Evelyn?'

'No.'

'Evelyn Keane. You'll find her.' There was a click.

Parker hung up, and a tractor trailer roared by, down-shifting as it went through the little town. It was the only traffic that had passed here since Parker had stopped the car. He stood in the phone-booth doorway now, and watched the truck taillights recede, the red lights outlining the trailer body. He frowned at the departing lights, thinking.

He had no way to get to Morris. No matter what means of transportation Keegan's killers were using, it made sense for them to work in a straight line, which would mean Detroit before the East Coast, starting from Minnesota. So there should be safe time for Claire in that. Maybe.

Parker went over and got into the Dodge and drove it back to the slot he'd stolen it from in the Minneapolis airport parking lot.

CHAPTER FIVE

There were no girls in the booths at this time of day, and no customers at the bar. When Parker walked in, the only person present was the bartender, writing on a sheet of paper beside the open cash register. Parker went over and sat on a stool, and the bartender looked sideways at him and said, 'I can't serve you a drink this early. Against the law.'

'I don't want a drink. I want a girl named Evelyn Keane.'

'Mrs. Keane? She isn't one of the girls here.'

'I don't want her for that. I want her because she knows how I can get in touch with a friend of mine.'

The bartender tapped the eraser of his pencil against his front teeth. 'I don't know her personally,' he said thoughtfully. 'I think

89

I may have heard the name. I could ask around.'

'Thanks.'

'I'll just make a couple phone calls. I can sell you a soda.'

'I don't need one.'

'Up to you. It just makes me nervous to have a John at the bar with no glass in front of him. I'll be right back.'

Parker read the bottle labels on the back bar for three minutes, and then the bartender came back with a folded piece of paper. 'I was told this was the place you ought to go.'

'Thanks.' Parker reached for his wallet.

'On the house,' the bartender said. 'Come back when you can buy me a drink.'

'Right.'

Parker went out and got a cab and took it to the address he'd been given, a brick apartment building constructed between the wars in a neighborhood that hadn't gotten better. There was no name in the slot next to the button for 5-F. Parker pushed it, waited to identify himself, and didn't have to; the buzzer sounded right away, unlocking the door.

There was no elevator, and 5-F was on the top floor. He went up, hearing nothing from the top of the stairwell, and walked along the carpeted corridor to the apartment door. Light bulbs imitating candle flames were in wall sconces imitating candles, but only three of them were lit, leaving the hall in semi-darkness.

Parker rang the bell, and the man who opened the door had a gun in his hand. 'Come in,' he said.

Parker held his hands out from his body, and went in.

There were four of them in the living room, but only one counted: the middle-aged fat man sitting on the sofa, rolling a cigar in his fingers. The other three, including the one who'd opened the door, were just hoods, extensions of the fat man's will.

The fat man said, 'Search him.'

Parker said, 'I have an automatic under my left arm and a knife under my collar in back.'

The fat man frowned at him and said nothing, while one of the hoods frisked him. He came up with the automatic and the knife, and put them on the console television set. Then he shook his head at the fat man, and stepped back out of the way.

The fat man said, 'What you got a knife down your back for?'

'In case somebody tells me to put my hands up.'

'You can draw and throw from back there?'

'Sometimes.'

'That's nice. What you want with Mrs. Keane?' He had a very slight accent, which made him sound thick-tongued.

'I'm looking for a friend of mine. I was told she knew where he was.'

91

'Who's the friend?'

'His name is Briley.'

The fat man looked at his hoods, then back at Parker. 'Briley? Who the hell is Briley?'

'Somebody I know, that I'm looking for. Another friend of his said I should ask Mrs. Keane.'

'Another friend. What other friend?'

'A man named Armwood, in Chicago.'

'Armwood?' The fat man was beginning to get angry, because he didn't understand what was going on and he felt frustrated. 'What the hell are all these names? Briley. Armwood. Who are *you*?'

'Tom Lynch.' That was the name on the documents in his wallet.

'Tom Lynch. Okay, Tom Lynch, she's right in there.' He nodded his head toward a closed door.

Parker went over and opened the door and she was lying on the bed in there. There were no lights on and the shade was drawn, but the window faced east and morning sunlight radiated through the shade, making an amber light. There was no question she was dead.

Parker shut the door again and turned to look at the fat man. 'I see.'

'Last night somebody did that. This morning you come looking.'

'Did they nail her to the wall?'

The fat man frowned. 'How do you mean, nail her to the wall?'

'With nails.'

'You mean for real? Like crucify? Why would anybody do a thing like that?'

'They got to another friend of mine two days ago. They nailed him to the wall.'

The fat man looked thoughtful, and then said. 'You connected with one of the families back East?'

'No, I'm on my own.'

'But you got friends.'

'Some.'

'And enemies. And they're killing your friends.'

'Yes.'

'Who are they?'

'I don't know. I'm behind them, and I'm trying to catch up.'

The fat man chewed the end of his cigar. It wasn't lit, but the end he was chewing gave off an odor. He took it from his mouth at last, gestured toward the closed door with it, and said, 'Mrs. Keane was a very important lady. You know what she did?'

'I think she ran girls.'

'She ran a *lot* of girls. She was very damn good. A woman is always better than a man at that, but it's tough to find a woman with business brains. They'd rather marry a man and steer him like a car.' He made steering motions over his stomach. He had a fat man's way of sitting, feet widespread and flat on the floor.

Parker waited. The fat man hadn't said anything yet that he should reply to, so he just stood there and waited.

The fat man brooded at the closed door, thinking about his organizational problems. Then he said, 'They're after you too, huh?'

'I think so. I can't be sure till I find them.'

'But you don't know who they are, or how come they're after you. You know how many?'

'Two, I think.'

'You can handle them yourself?'

'I think so.'

The fat man nodded his head at the three hoods. 'You want me to loan you a boy?'

'I'm better off on my own.'

'This thing ought to be punished. They left me one hell of a headache. I figured to start my own people out.'

'They wouldn't know where to go or what to look for.'

'That's where you could help them,' the fat man said.

'I'm better off by myself.'

The fat man pursed his lips. 'Look,' he said. 'If Mrs. Keane knew this friend of yours, Briley, it means she supplied him girls. So what I can do now, I can put some people to work on the phone, check out all her girls, find out who got sent to a guy named Briley. Then I can tell you where he is. Or on the other hand, I can send people of my own and

94

the hell with you.'

'Briley doesn't know your people. He knows me. He'll believe me and work with me. If we aren't wasting too much time here.'

'Time. Aldo, call the office for me. Lynch, go sit down over there.'

Parker went over to the chair in the corner and sat down. The way the room was arranged, all four of them were now between him and his armaments on top of the television set.

Aldo dialed the phone, talked into it briefly, handed the receiver to the fat man. The fat man rumbled into it for a while, then hung up. 'Lynch, come over here.'

Parker walked over.

'Lynch, we decided to save our own manpower. You want to take care of them, you take care of them. You wait here now, somebody will call you. Lynch, you need help, you lose the trail, anything goes wrong, call Aldo.'

The card said, *Family Bowling Center*, with a Dearborn address and phone number. Parker put it in his pocket.

The fat man heaved himself to his feet. 'Don't go over to your gun till after we leave.' He walked toward the door, the three hoods around him like tugboats around an ocean liner. At the door, he looked back and said, 'Have a good hunt.'

'Thank you.'

They left. Parker glanced at the closed bedroom door, then went over and got the automatic and knife and put them away.

There was the possibility he was simply being set up to eat this rap, though it seemed pointless. Still the chance existed that the fat man would have Aldo dial Police Headquarters from some other telephone, and in five or ten minutes the law would walk in and start asking questions Parker couldn't answer.

None of the apartment windows overlooked the street. Parker propped the hall door open with a straight chair from the kitchen and walked down the corridor past the stairwell to the window at the end. Down below was the sidewalk and the street. Across the way, two of the hoods were helping the fat man into the back of a black Cadillac. Parker watched the three of them drive away. It didn't surprise him that the fourth had been left behind; he'd expected the fat man would tie shadow to him until he got to the people who'd killed Mrs. Keane. It was a problem that could be handled later.

He waited half an hour. This was a workingmen's apartment house, and though there was occasional movement on the floors below, no one appeared up on the top floor at all. And then, after half an hour by the window overlooking the street, Parker heard the phone ring in Mrs. Keane's apartment.

He strode down the corridor, shoved the chair out of the way so the door would swing closed, and crossed the room to pick up the receiver.

A colorless female voice said, 'Robin Hood Motel, Pontiac.'

CHAPTER SIX

The third time Parker pounded on the door, a sleep-heavy man in T-shirt and jockey shorts opened it and blinked blearily out at him, weaving slightly as he said, 'What day is it?'

'I'm looking for Briley.'

'Briley? Christ, is that the sun?'

Parker pushed the door the rest of the way open and went in. The sleepy man tottered backward, not quite losing his balance, saying, 'Jesus, fella, don't knock a fella over.'

Briley's group had a four-unit separate section of the motel completely to themselves. This section was off behind the parking lot, where they wouldn't disturb anybody. All the connecting doors were open, the drapes were closed over all the windows, and they had their own private dim-lit world in which to party.

A naked girl was curled up asleep on the floor in front of the television set, which was showing a soap opera with the sound turned off. Two fretful women sat at a kitchen table on the grainy screen and mouthed worried remarks at one another.

A couple was asleep in one of the room's double beds; the other was empty, but rumpled. Empty bottles, full ashtrays, and stray playing cards were all over the room. The girl sleeping in front of the television set was clutching a thick white candle in one hand.

Parker went over to look at the man asleep in the bed, but it wasn't Briley. He turned back to the one who was semi-awake and said, 'Briley's the one I want to see.'

'It's got to be too early in the day. What did I do with my watch?'

Parker went over and took him by the upper arm and applied pressure. 'Briley,' he said. 'Where's Briley?'

'Jesus! He's down at the end! I told you twice already, down in the end room!'

Parker released him. 'Thanks.'

'One thing,' the man said, and waved in the general direction of the girl on the floor. 'That one's mine.' Then he weaved over and got into bed with the other couple, and began rummaging with the girl's body under the sheet. Eyes closed, she rolled over to face him and put her arms around him, and when Parker left the room they were moving together, neither of them entirely awake.

Briley wasn't in the last room. The ones in

between had continued the same general style as the first one, and unit four was no exception, except that in here there was an odd number of people; a man and woman asleep in one bed, and a woman asleep alone in the other.

It took a while to wake the solitary woman. Parker finally took a warm bottle of club soda and emptied it on her. She sat up, then, sputtering, shaking, and Parker said, 'Where's Briley?'

'What?' She used the sheet to wipe her face. 'Oog. I hate soda.'

'Briley,' Parker said.

'He got a phone call,' she said. 'He went away.'

'Where?'

'How do I know? He wrote something down over there.'

'What time did he get the call?'

She peered up at him, squinting although the room was very dim. 'Are you kidding?'

Parker left her and went over to the stand between the beds. The phone was there, and a pencil, and a small memo pad of blank white paper.

The woman patted the wet pillow. 'What a hell of a mess you made in here. That wasn't nice.'

Parker picked up the pad and pencil and walked around the beds and went into the john. He turned on the light and shut the door, and tried to angle the pad so he could read the instructions in the top sheet that had been left when Briley had written on the sheet above it. He could see the lines, but he couldn't make them out.

There was a formica counter beside the sink. Parker put the pad down on that and very lightly brushed the pencil back and forth over the paper. The indented lines grew less dark. The scrawled note read: '53 2 mi N Romeo left church Galt on right.' Parker put the pad and pencil in his pocket, opened the door, switched off the bathroom light, and went outside to find a man dressed in nothing but pants blocking his way with a bottle in his hand, the bottle held as a club.

The man said, 'What's your story, Mac?'

'I'm a friend of Briley's.'

'He ain't here.'

'I know that.' The woman he'd awakened was asleep again, her head on the wet pillow. Both women were asleep.

'Then you oughta get outa here.'

Parker said nothing. He started for the door, passing to the man's left. He went one pace farther, then dropped to one knee and the bottle curved over his head, the man grunting as the swing went past the spot where he'd expected it to stop. Parker came up behind the swing and hit the man twice in the stomach. A man who's been partying has a weak stomach. The man made a sound, dropped the bottle, backed up two steps, ran into his bed, and fell down on it, both arms over his stomach. He landed on his woman's legs, and she began to thrash around in her sleep. The man rolled over onto his side on the bed and stayed there, his arms still pressed to his stomach, his mouth open like a fish.

Parker went outside, where the sun seemed twice as bright as before, glaring off the concrete drive. Over on Route 59, trucks were going by, smudging the air.

The car he'd picked up in Detroit, a green Mustang, was down at the other end of this four-unit section. Parker walked down to it, got in, and drove a quarter mile to a gas station. He looked at a Michigan map while the tank was being filled. There was a Route 53. North of Detroit on 53 was a town called Romeo.

When he pulled out of the gas station, the beige Buick that had been following him since Mrs. Keane's place was still behind him.

CHAPTER SEVEN

Parker slowed for the turn. He was nowhere near Romeo or Route 53. He was turning from a blacktop secondary road onto a dirt road that led directly into woods. The beige

Buick, because of the lack of other traffic out here, was keeping well back.

Parker drove half a mile before he found a place where he could pull the Mustang off the dirt track. Trees hemmed the car in on all sides. It was green, which in here was a lucky color.

Parker left the car, crossed the dirt road, and made his way through the trees back the way he'd come, paralleling the path. After a minute or two he heard the Buick coming, and stopped beside a tree. His automatic was in his right hand.

The Buick went slowly by, crumpling twigs beneath the tires. The driver was one of the hoods who'd been with the fat man. The one beside him, Parker had never seen before, but he was in the same mold.

Parker shot the left front tire, and waited, and for a long time nothing happened at all. The driver had stopped the car the instant the shot sounded, the man beside him was holding a revolver up with its butt resting on the dashboard, and both were turning their heads, looking at the woods all around them. Neither tried to hide, neither made any move to get out of the car. It was a very cool, very contained reaction.

Parker called, 'Drive forward. Very slowly.'

They both looked toward the sound of his voice, but he knew they couldn't see him. He waited while they looked for him, then looked at one another, and finally the driver put the car in gear and it slid forward, the hood bumping up and down because of the flat tire.

The car went just a few feet, and then the brake lights went on and it stopped again. The driver called, 'We've got a flat.'

'Drive anyway. Slowly.'

The driver looked irritable, but he took his foot off the brake and the Buick limped forward again.

Parker kept to the trees, far enough away so he'd be difficult to see as he moved from cover to cover, yet close enough to keep the Buick in sight. He didn't want the passenger to slip out and come looking for him on his blind side.

The brake lights went on again briefly when they came to the Mustang, but the car didn't entirely stop. Parker angled in closer, and when the Buick had gone about thirty feet past the Mustang, he called, 'Stop there,' and the Buick stopped. 'Turn off the engine. Climb out. Both on the left side. Leave your guns on the front seat. Walk around in front of the car. Face away from the car. Put your hands on your heads.'

Parker moved cautiously to the Buick, watching them. Neither of them said anything, to him or to one another. He opened the driver's door, took the keys out of the ignition, put them in his pocket. There were two revolvers on the seat. He put away his own automatic, picked up the two revolvers, stepped back from the car, and said, 'You'll hear shots now. I'm shooting tires, not you.'

'And you're making a big mistake,' the driver said.

'Before you shoot the tires—' the other one said, and Parker put a bullet in the left rear. As he walked around the back of the car, the second man started again: 'We're along to back you up. You're putting heat on yourself for no reason, you aren't what we're after.'

'I told your boss I work alone.' Parker shot the right rear tire, moved up the side of the car.

The driver said, 'Don't you know we're national? Don't you know you can't go anywhere we won't find you?'

Parker shot the fourth tire. 'Take five paces forward.'

They moved forward. The driver said, 'You're going out of your way to make a lot of people mad at you.'

'One pace to the right. Now lie down. Face-down.'

They were now where he could keep an eye on them while he backed up the Mustang. He had to lose sight of them for a few seconds while he got into the car and started the engine, and when he backed onto the road, one of them was out of sight and the other was on his feet. Parker ignored that, and ran the Mustang in reverse all the way to the blacktop road, where he turned north.

CHAPTER EIGHT

Glass shattered in front of his face; a pistol shot sounded in the tall reeds beside the house. Parker leaped over the porch railing, landed on his shoulder, and rolled for cover over the brown-earth yard. In scraggly underbrush, he took out his automatic, got to hands and knees, and crawled for the back of the house.

He was going down the right side of the building, and the shot had come from the swampy ground off to the left. If the sniper didn't move before Parker got there, he'd be flanked when Parker came around the rear of the house and moved into the area of the swamp.

There was no other sound, no other movement. This farmhouse, several miles northwest of Romeo on an unnumbered gravel road, had a battered old rural delivery mailbox out front with the name *Galt* on it, but gave the impression of having been deserted for at least a few years. Most of the windows had been broken, and somebody had removed clapboard siding from one section of the side wall. There were no other houses in sight.

It was now midafternoon, and as hot as it was going to get today, possibly sixty degrees. Mayflies made a background blur of sound that only intensified the silence; it was as though the leaves could be heard rustling on the fat oak trees beyond the farmer's field.

Parker came around the rear of the house, and stopped when he was still in cover but could see the Mustang where he'd parked it in front of the porch. He waited, sitting on his heels, ready to jump in any direction, and nothing happened, nobody moved. A slight breeze semaphored tree leaves all around. Behind the broken windows of the house were no curtains or lights, only darkness and vaguely seen blank walls with rectangular door spaces.

Parker moved. The ground underfoot was very soft; water squeezed to the surface around his shoes when he shifted his weight. He moved in a crouch, with one hand touching the ground for balance, and the sensation against those fingers was cold and damp.

Movement. A rustling. Reeds bent, sluggishly, and didn't come upright again. Parker watched the movement to his right, away from the house, and waited for it to become something meaningful, but after a few minutes it stopped again.

He headed toward where the agitation had been, and through the reeds he saw a form stretched out on the ground, and when he came closer, it was a man lying face-down, arms bent laxly around his head.

Alone? Parker circled him, listening, watching, and when the silence continued to stretch without snapping, he moved in closer and saw the automatic enclosed in the slack fingers of the man's right hand. And also the familiar contour of his head, a reminiscent slope to the shoulder and back.

Parker stood upright, and looked around, and nothing happened. He stepped quickly forward and kicked the barrel of the gun, and it slid away through the reeds with a faint squishing sound.

Parker bent and turned Briley over, and the front of his shirt and trousers was smeared with mud and blood, drying unevenly together. He put his hand to Briley's throat and felt pulse, felt breath shuddering in and out. He got to his feet, looked around, listened, then stepped to the left, bent, picked up Briley's gun, held it in his hand and looked at it.

It wasn't the same automatic he'd carried in the robbery. This one was a Colt Super Auto, chambered for high-speed .38's; a fairly old, well-used gun, it had the scratches and scars of a weapon that had been through many hands. Parker ejected the clip, and it was half empty. He put the clip back, felt the front of the barrel, and it was warm.

Leaving Briley where he was, Parker went back to the house and up on the porch. Briley's shot had further broken the broken glass in the storm door and had then gouged a new streak in the graying wood of the main door, before digging a hole for itself in the frame. Parker pulled open the storm door and saw the jimmy marks on the frame near the inner door's knob. He pushed, and the door eased open. Holding his own gun in his right hand and Briley's Colt in his left, he kicked the door open farther, and stepped in.

The place had been stripped. Wiring straggled from the walls where light switches and outlets had been removed. Molding around windows and doors had been stripped away, and even part of the living-room floor had been ripped up and taken away, leaving a grave-size hole through which a dirt-floored basement could be seen.

There was nobody around. Half a dozen cigarette butts near the living room's front window showed where they'd stood while they'd waited for Briley to get here. And a piece of paper near them on the floor seemed newer than the general layer of scag around the place. Parker picked it up and it had printing on it in two places. In one place, *The Hearth*, *Los Angeles*, *California—Where Beef Is King*, and in the other place, *American*

Sugar Refining Company, New York, N. Y.
The paper had been wrapped around a cube
of sugar, and carried to Detroit from Los
Angeles.

Parker frowned at the paper, turning it in
his hands. Sugar cubes made him think of
horses; people gave cubes of sugar to horses.
But why have sugar here? Then, still
thinking, *horse* made him think of the other
way the word was used: horse means heroin.
But sugar has nothing to do with heroin,
except sometimes wholesalers use sugar to cut
horse.

And then the thought of heroin led him to
the next step, and he knew what the sugar
was here for. He held the piece of paper up
toward the light, over facing the broken-out
windows, and there was the small hole, the
pinprick in the paper. Needle-prick.

He threw the paper away and went outside
again and back over to Briley, who hadn't
moved. He put his hand to Briley's throat,
and the pulse was still working, though very
feebly. Having turned Briley over before,
Parker had made the bleeding from his
stomach increase again.

It was clear what had happened. Briley had
come here, the two waiting for him had
tipped their hands too soon, Briley had run
for cover. They'd managed to hit him with
one or more shots before he got clear of them,
but he'd kept going and either held them off

or lost them in those woods over there. So they'd given up after a while, and they'd gone away, taking Briley's car with them. Briley had come back to the house and passed out, and the sound of Parker's car arriving had brought him back to consciousness one last time. He'd come partly awake, afraid they were back again, and fired at the figure he'd seen on the porch. But that had been it for him, and he'd faded out again, and now he was finished.

There was no point trying to get Briley conscious again, and even if there'd been a reason for it, Parker doubted it would be possible. Briley was dead everywhere but his lungs; they still kept moving the air in and out. But not for any good reason, and not for long.

Parker got to his feet again, smeared Briley's Colt with his palms to obscure his prints, dropped the gun on the ground beside the curved-fingered hand, and went away to the Mustang.

Seven miles from the farmhouse, he stopped at a diner, ordered lunch, and got two dollars in change from the cashier, which he took to the phone booth back by the rest rooms. He dialed Claire's number in New Jersey, paid the operator what she asked for when she came on, and listened to three rings before Claire's voice said, 'Hello?'

'Hello, it's me.'

'Oh,' she said. 'Mr. Parker. Yes, I've been expecting you to call.' She didn't sound frightened at all.

PART THREE

CHAPTER ONE

Claire stood in front of the house. She was wearing a pale green man-style shirt, and it wasn't enough; she was cold, and stood with her arms folded around herself, shoulders hunched.

It was Sunday, shortly after noon, twenty minutes after the call from Handy McKay. Claire stood there and watched Parker open the farther garage doors and go inside to his car. How could he travel that way, without any luggage at all, nothing, not even an overnight bag? She thought, *Are we as mysterious to them as they are to us?* She stroked her cupped palms up and down over her upper arms, to warm herself, and thought briefly of her dead husband, who had been named Edward and called Ed. He'd always traveled with a black attaché case. She'd hated it, it had destroyed the glamour of the commercial pilot's uniform he'd worn, it made everything mundane.

The Pontiac backed out of the garage and made a tight backward U-turn. When it stopped, the left side of the car was toward her. Parker had his window rolled down, and he called, 'I'll phone you. Tonight sometime.'

'Good.' She raised a hand to wave, the way she used to do with Ed, and realized a second too late that with this one the gesture was inappropriate. She let her hand fall again, awkwardly, the flow of the movement interrupted, and finding no words to seam the awkwardness, nodded instead.

The Pontiac rolled down the driveway and turned right on the blacktop road. Claire stood in front of the house, rubbing her folded arms, watching the car, and when it disappeared she flashed a sudden broad smile, unintended, and into her mind came the thought, *Now it's really mine!*

She pushed the smile and the thought away, and turned to go into the house and distract herself with the busy-work of making a pot of tea to take off the chill, but she knew what the smile meant, and what the thought meant, and she knew they were both true.

· They meant the house was different now, and it *was* different. She went in and stood in the kitchen a minute before starting the water for tea, and the house had a different kind of silence about it now. Different from last week, before Parker had come here for the first time. In the days between her moving into the house and his arrival, it had simply been a house that a solitary woman had bought and was living in alone. During the four days of his stay, it had been *their* house, which meant nobody's house; it was simply where they were staying, like a hotel room. But now, with his mark on the place but with him not here, it was the house in which she waited for her man. That made all the difference in the world.

She drank a cup of tea in the living room. The chairs faced the fireplace, but she turned one of them around to face the windows instead, with their view of the lake. She sat and looked at the empty lake and the tiny dots that were empty houses on the opposite shore, and the green mountains in the background, and she thought she would probably not want to stay here in the summer, when the lake and those houses would be full. They would spend the summer somewhere exciting, New York or San Francisco. Maybe they could go to Europe.

Twelve thousand dollars. Not very much, really, he usually made more than that in one of his jobs. But he'd do more.

There came into her mind, all at once, the remembered picture of Lempke, his face all bloody, coming through the hole in the bourse room wall and saying, 'French.' As though it were a surprising word he'd just invented, and not the name of the man who had just shot and killed him.

She hated the memory. It was brief, and vivid, and incomplete, and always terrifying. In her memory Lempke came through the wall and said, 'French,' and his face was bloody, and he was in the process of dying. But in her memory he never fell.

Lempke and Parker and some others had been doing a 'job,' that strangely inappropriate word Parker used for his robberies. It was a coin convention, and they were stealing the cased coins from the guarded room where they were being held overnight. A coin dealer named Billy Lebatard, distantly related by marriage to Claire's dead husband, had conceived the robbery, hoping the money from it would win him Claire. It wouldn't, but she'd let him believe it might; this was shortly after Ed had been killed in the plane crash, and shortly after she'd learned just how little he had left her to go on with.

It had still been a game, then. Everything in her life up to that point had been a game, one way or another. The teasing boy-girl game that had seemed glamorous and fun in her teens, the exciting-life game in being the woman of an exciting man—Andy, the stock-car racer; Ed; the others in between—and after the death of Ed, a new game, charming con-woman, with Billy Lebatard as her first fun victim.

And in the middle of it all, in the middle of the robbery that she had instigated, suddenly the game had stopped and humorless deadly people who weren't playing at anything had taken over, and Lempke had come through a hole in the wall with blood all over his face.

Parker could have left her there, then. She

had screamed, and then she had become helpless, unable to think or to move or to do anything to save herself. He had gotten her out, she still didn't know how, and when she had gotten control of her mind again, she'd felt nothing but terror and guilt. Lempke was dead. Billy Lebatard was dead. The game had crashed, and she had no idea what to do next, where to go, how to breathe. She'd said to Parker, 'Will you take me with you?' and he'd said, 'For how long?' and she'd known enough to say, 'Until one of us gets bored, I suppose.' Later she'd said to him, 'I know sometimes you'll have to go away and do these things, but those times you can't talk about. Not tell me anything, not before, not after.' He'd said, 'That's how I'd be. Whether you wanted it or not.'

Four years now. Living in hotels, mostly, Parker away occasionally, with her most of the time. But even when he was with her, he was in some manner away from her; he was the most locked-in man she'd ever met. And even when he was away, he was in some manner with her, because his existence was letting her go on playing the exciting-life game after all, with added safety rules. It was exciting to eat in a restaurant with him and know she was the only one aware of who and what he was, and by some strange extension it became exciting to eat in a restaurant alone and know none of the people around her

119

could guess what kind of man she was waiting for.

But even with the added safety rules, there had been an undercurrent of nervousness in her life that had refused to go away. She'd expected it to go with time, the occasional dreams about Lempke's face, the hollow feeling of darkness in the middle of sunny days, but it had neither lessened nor increased in the four years, remaining an ever-present knot of tension in the back of her mind.

She hadn't told Parker about it, partly because she wasn't sure what his reaction would be and partly because in putting the nervousness and fear into words she was afraid she would make them stronger. But she'd tried to find something to ease the pressure, and when the thought of a house had come to her, a base of operations, a solid real dependable home which would be *hers*, she had known at once it was the answer.

There had been a secret pleasure in the conversations with real estate agents, listening to their talk of taxes and schools, knowing they would never guess the real priorities inside her head. Living her true life below the placid surface of an assumed life; that was her joy.

And now she had it. The house, the nest, forming the frame of her existence, and outside it the man who gave that existence its texture. Every task, no matter how ordinary, became charged with another level of meaning when she was doing it *while waiting for Parker*.

Waiting for Parker. The thought of that made her remember the other thing he'd told her she was waiting for; whoever had wanted to know where Parker could be found would probably be coming here. If Parker didn't get to them first.

He would, wouldn't he? She frowned, looking out at the lake, considering the possibilities for the first time. There was a wind across the lake, the water was choppy; it looked cold.

Would some stranger be coming here? She hadn't wanted to think about that, not with Parker telling her to leave her house and go back to a hotel, but now that he was gone and the pressure on her to leave had gone with him, it was possible to think, to consider the likelihood that someone from Parker's unknowable and menacing world might be coming here for reasons she knew nothing about.

The afternoon was edging by, the quality of the light was changing on the lake. She felt she should make some movement, some preparation, do something to guard herself and her house from intruders.

The last mouthful of tea in the cup was cold. She made a face, got to her feet, carried the empty cup to the kitchen. There was still more in the pot, but it was only lukewarm. She didn't want it, anyway. She put on a jacket, walked around the house locking windows and doors, and then went out to the garage and opened the doors and backed the blue Buick out. And then discovered there was no way to lock the garage doors. There was a hasp lock but no padlock to secure it. Irritated, blaming the real estate man in some obscure fashion, she got into the Buick and drove away.

There was a town three miles away, but it was very small, too small for what she wanted. The nearest town of any size was twelve miles farther on.

Her first stop was a hardware store, where she bought two padlocks, one for each set of garage doors. She also looked in their phone book, and found a nearby sporting-goods store.

At first she wasn't sure she'd come to the right place. Fishing equipment was everywhere, from racks of rods to nets hanging on the walls to display cases full of lures to creels hanging from the ceiling. The short round man who came swimming through all this toward her looked like the fish it was all designed for, with his round bald head and light-reflecting glasses. 'Yes, miss.' He had a habit of rubbing his hands together, which gave the impression he planned to cheat somehow.

She said, 'My husband wants me to go hunting with him, so I have to have my own rifle. You do sell rifles?'

'Certainly, certainly. This way, please.'

A doorway in the back of the store, hemmed in with fishing net, led to an entirely different world. Rifles and pistols were everywhere, intermixed with red or red-and-black hunter's clothing. There were large pictures of animals on the walls; elk, deer, moose.

'Mr. Amberville? Mr. Amberville, this young lady would like to buy a rifle. Mr. Amberville will take care of you, miss.'

The fish-man went back to his own department, and Mr. Amberville came smiling over. A younger man, very thin, he had the bony features of an Austrian ski instructor. He seemed pleasant, but remote; he said, 'A rifle? A present?'

'No, for myself. My husband wants me to go hunting with him, so I have to have a rifle of my own.'

'I see.' He looked her up and down, impersonally, as though he were about to sell her a coat. 'Something light,' he said. 'What will you be going after?'

'I beg your pardon?'

'What game will you be hunting?'

'Oh.' What was man-size? 'Deer, I suppose.'

He said, 'Hmmm. Well, let's see. Over this way.'

He began to show her rifles. She held them, and they all seemed heavy and awkward and unusable in her hands. He stood beside her, talking, pointing out the fine points of the different rifles as she held them, and she had no idea what he was talking about.

She was beginning to get discouraged. She looked around, and saw some other rifles in another case, and said, 'What are those?'

'Twenty-twos,' he said. 'A little light for what you have in mind.'

'Let me see them,' she said. 'They look more my size.'

'They're not really the best for deer-hunting,' he said, frowning. 'They're what you'd want for small game.'

'That's all right, I don't expect to hit anything, anyway.'

He didn't seem to like that, but he didn't say anything. Silently he put away the rifles he'd been showing her and led her over to the other case.

'That one,' she said, picking one of them almost at random, simply on the basis of looks.

His expression doubtful, he opened the case and took down the rifle she'd pointed to. 'This is the Marlin 39A,' he said. 'It holds twenty-five shorts, twenty longs, or eighteen long rifles. It's forty and a half inches long, weighs six and three quarter pounds. It's lever-action; like this.' His right hand made a fast down-and-up motion with a metal loop on the bottom of the rifle, making click sounds.

She said, 'What's that for?'

'It chambers your cartridge.' At her expression, he pointed to the smaller barrel under the main barrel. 'You load the rounds in here. The lever—'

'You mean the bullets.'

'That's right, the bullets. You load them in front here. The lever brings one bullet up into firing position, and ejects the used casing from the bullet you've already fired.'

'You mean I have to do that with the lever every time I shoot.'

'That's right.'

'May I—?'

She took the rifle, and tried the lever, and didn't like it. 'No, that's not for me.' She looked at the other rifles in the case.

'If I may suggest—'

'Yes, of course.'

He put the Marlin away and brought out a different gun. 'This is the Remington 66. It holds fifteen long rifles. Those are the bullets. It's thirty-eight and a half inches long and weighs four pounds.'

'What do I have to do to get the bullet ready for fire?'

'Nothing. It's auto-load.'

'May I see it?'

'Of course.'

It was the lightest rifle so far, and also the shortest. She was too self-conscious to hold it up to her shoulder and look down the sights, but of them all, this rifle felt the least cumbersome in her hands. 'I'll take it,' she said.

'Very good. And ammunition?'

'Please.'

The rifle was fifty-four dollars and fifty cents—he wanted to sell her a four-power telescopic sight as well, which she refused—and a box of fifty long rifle .22 caliber bullets was eighty-five cents. She paid in cash, and he carried the cardboard carton with the rifle in it out to the car for her.

Driving back, she suddenly found herself afraid that Parker's enemies would be waiting for her at the house, and she felt an abrupt deep wave of resentment at him for endangering her home this way. The feeling of resentment didn't last, but the fear did, and two miles from the house she pulled off the road and took the rifle out of the carton.

She spent fifteen minutes parked off the road, studying the weapon, reading the instruction booklet that had come with it, and very gingerly loading it. She put it down on the back seat, barrel pointing at the right-hand door, and after that, drove much more slowly and cautiously, afraid that a bump in the road would make the thing fire.

There was no one at the house. She fastened both sets of garage doors with the new padlocks, then went in through the kitchen and down the hall and used the interior door to get into the garage again and get the rifle. After not being sure what to do with it at first, she put it down on the sofa in the living room.

She looked at the phone, but it didn't ring.

CHAPTER TWO

Claire fired, and the rifle stock thumped hard into her right shoulder. She grimaced, and stepped backward away from the pain, and held the rifle with her right hand so she could rub her shoulder with the left. She hadn't expected the rifle to do anything like that, and the surprise and hurt distracted her for a minute from looking to see whether or not she'd hit her target.

It was a pint milk carton—a half-and-half carton, really—that she'd put on the ground in the middle of the backyard, between the house and the lake. She'd stood up on the porch, in the doorway, and aimed carefully at the cow on the carton, and very slowly squeezed the trigger.

And she'd missed. Coming down from the porch, she looked at the carton to find it untouched, and the ground around it also untouched. She frowned at that, and ranged wider, and could see absolutely no sign of the bullet anywhere at all.

Hadn't it fired? The rifle had punched her in the shoulder, and she remembered from the Remington instruction booklet that that was called recoil. But had it been more recoil than normal, and was that because the bullet had somehow gotten jammed inside the barrel? She almost looked in the barrel to see, but recognized what that picture would look like from cartoons in magazines, and refrained.

She stood in the yard, holding the rifle in both hands, looking this way and that like a pioneer woman searching for Indians, and then noticed the window in the side wall of the boathouse. It had twelve smallish panes, three across and four down. She put the rifle to her shoulder again and peered down over the sights at the bottom middle pane.

As she started to squeeze the trigger, she felt her shoulder shrinking away from the rifle butt. That was no good, she knew that much. She pulled the rifle hard into her shoulder with her left hand, kept squinting one-eyed at the bottom middle pane, and fired.

It bucked less this time. Also, she noticed it less because she heard the tinkle of broken

128

glass. Elated, she hurried over to the boathouse and discovered a triangular section of glass gone from the top right pane. 'High and to the right,' she muttered. By about three feet.

But at least the rifle was working. And with a little more practice, she expected to get pretty good at it.

But she couldn't keep shooting out windowpanes. She looked around again, saw nothing helpful, then put the rifle down on the grass and ran into the house. In the kitchen she got a package of paper plates and a cardboard of thumbtacks. As an afterthought, she grabbed the pencil from the window sill over the sink. Outside again, she tacked the paper plates to the side of the boathouse in the vague shape of a man, stood back about twenty feet, and fired at his head.

The next four shots were all high and to the right, but each of them was closer to the paper plates. She was beginning to see that it was the recoil that was throwing her aim off, that and the way she pulled the trigger. The recoil made the rifle barrel lift upward, and her manner of pulling the trigger made the barrel veer to the right. She concentrated on keeping the barrel down and her right hand still, and the next shot nicked the upper right edge of the paper plate. Pleased with herself, she walked over and wrote the number 1 on the plate next to the ragged hole.

In all, she used thirty rounds, twenty-eight of them at the paper plates, nineteen of them hitting the plates, the last ten in a row all hitting home. The sun was going down behind the mountains across the lake when she took the plates and thumbtacks down from the wall and carried them with the rifle and the ammunition carton back into the house. She locked the door behind herself, leaned the rifle against the wall near the fireplace, started a fire, and went out to the kitchen to make dinner. She turned on the kitchen radio and sang with the music.

CHAPTER THREE

When the phone rang, shortly after two in the morning, she was just getting into bed. There were two extensions, one in the living room and one here, on the nightstand on her side of the bed. She picked it up after one ring, and said, 'Hello?'

Parker's voice: 'It's me. How are things?'

'Fine.' She used her free hand to lean a pillow up against the headboard, then rested her back against it. She was wearing a yellow nightgown he'd never seen; when they were together, she slept nude. She said, 'How are you?'

'No visitors?'

'Nobody at all,' she said. Out in the living room, the dying fire made a dry settling sound. 'Will you be back soon?'

'My friend died of a lingering illness,' he said. His voice was as flat and emotionless as ever. 'Very painful illness.'

It took her a second to understand his meaning, and when she did she didn't like it. 'Oh,' she said. She knew what he was going to say next, and was already rejecting it.

She was right. He said, 'You ought to take a day or two off. Go to New York, do some shopping.'

The mulish feeling came over her again; she could feel it even in the set of her jaw. 'I don't want to leave my house,' she said.

'This is serious!' His voice wasn't more emotional, exactly, merely more intense, pushing each word harder into her ear.

'So am I,' she said. And then, casting around to find something reassuring to say to him, heard herself add, 'Tomorrow I'll buy a dog.' Which she'd had no intention of doing, till now. But a dog might be nice, a companion during the times when Parker was away.

He was saying, 'I'm talking about tonight.'

'I'll be all right. I went out and got a rifle.'

She hadn't intended to tell him that, not until afterward, when he was here again and this situation was finished. It sounded foolish, really, to say she'd bought a rifle; she

131

wouldn't tell him about the time this afternoon spent shooting at paper plates out by the lake.

There was a little silence from his end of the wire now, and she read it to mean that the rifle hadn't reassured him any more than the dog had, and that he was trying to find some way to change her mind. But in the end all he did was repeat himself: 'I think you ought to go away.'

She didn't want him to say that any more. 'I know what you think,' she said, more sharply than she'd intended, and tried at once to soften it, saying, 'I know you're worried about me. But you just don't know what this house means to me. I *can't* go away from it, not after I just got into it. I won't be *driven* away from it.'

She felt she had told him a great deal about herself then, much more than was usual to her nature. She felt almost frightened, wondering what he would do with what she'd said, and the silence from the phone extended this time, and he did nothing with it, and finally she said, hesitantly, 'Hello? Are you there?'

'I'm here.' He said it distractedly, and then there was silence again, and when next he spoke, his voice was matter of fact, seamless again, without the increase in pressure. 'What you do right now,' he said, 'you pack everything there that's mine and get it out.

Stow it all in one of the empty houses around there. But do it now, don't wait till morning.'

'You don't have that much here,' she said. Looking around the dimlit bedroom, all she saw of his was one pair of shoes on the floor near the closet.

'So it won't take long,' he said. 'If anybody comes looking for me, you don't fight them. Understand me? You don't fight them.'

She felt herself getting mulish again, thinking of the practice time with the rifle, but she fought the mulish feeling down and said. 'What do I do instead?'

'Tell them you just run a message service, you only see me two or three times a year, when I give you some money for taking care of my messages. What you tell them, any time a message comes for me you call the Wilmington Hotel in New York and leave it for me in the name of Edward Latham. You got that?'

'Yes. But what—'

'Give me the names back.'

She hadn't been paying particular attention to the names, not knowing they meant anything. She said, 'Is it important?'

'Yes. Those are the names to use.'

'Wilmington Hotel,' she said, trying to remember. 'Edward—I'm sorry.'

'Latham. Edward Latham.'

'Edward Latham. Is that all?'

'Don't antagonize them. They're very

mean people.'

The very flatness of the statement made her believe him. 'I know how to be a little mouse,' she said, remembering times when she'd fought male strength with female cunning, feeling strong in the memories.

'That's good,' he said. 'I'll get back there as soon as I can.'

It was rare that he let her feel tender toward him. 'I know you will,' she said.

'Clean my stuff out of there right away.'

'I will.'

She heard the click as he hung up, but held the phone to her ear a second or so longer, then reluctantly put it back in its cradle.

Get his things out of here. It was after two in the morning, she was ready for bed, the temptation was strong to let it go until morning. But she believed him about the people he was involved with, and she believed he knew best how to prepare for them. Reluctant, but dogged, she got out of bed again, turned on the overhead light, and got his suitcase from the closet.

One suitcase was all it took; that, and fifteen minutes. Then she dressed, putting clothes on over the nightgown, and lugged the suitcase through the kitchen and out of the house.

It was very dark out, patches of cloud in the sky, no moon. She stood on the gravel a minute, then put the suitcase down, went back into the house, and got the flashlight from its kitchen drawer.

Stow his things in an empty house, he'd said. The houses were empty on both sides, why not pick one of them? She shone the flashlight right and left, and chose the house to her left because there seemed to be fewer trees and bushes in the way.

She left the suitcase outside the lake-side door, and went around the house trying doors and windows, all of which were locked. Finally she broke a window on the side opposite her own house, unlocked it, raised it, and climbed in. The electricity was turned off, so she found her way through to the rear door by flashlight, unlocked it, opened it, and brought the suitcase inside. The bedroom closet seemed a perfectly adequate place to leave it. She went out by the door, leaving it unlocked, and went back across to her own place and inside, carefully locking the door behind her.

In bed again, in the darkness, the rifle on the floor under the bed, she lay gazing at the paler rectangle of the window and thought about Parker, and began to think sexually about Parker. She was lying on her back, but the sexual images involving Parker grew so insistent she rolled over on her side, trying to find a position without sexual connotations.

It was strange, this feeling. When she was involved with a man, and he was with her, she had very strong and healthy sex urges, but when she was alone, she never thought very much about sex at all. She had always been glad to welcome Parker back after one of his jobs, because his own sexual appetites were always at their strongest then, but the time spent waiting was usually empty of sexual frustration. Yet tonight her mind was crowded with remembered incidents, moments, expressions, and she couldn't get rid of them, couldn't get to sleep.

After a long while the window rectangle began to lighten. 'This is ridiculous,' she said, aloud, and got out of bed. She went to the kitchen and brought back the radio and turned on an all-night music station from New York. Listening to the music, the announcer, the commercials, she finally began to relax toward sleep. During the five A.M. news her mind at last shut down and she slept. And in her dreams Parker mounted her and stroked long and deep and endless, and it kept being spoiled for her because there was someone else just over his shoulder.

CHAPTER FOUR

None of the dogs were any good. Today was Sunday, so no pet shops were open, and Claire had been limited to the private owners advertising in the local Sunday paper. Most of the dogs listed were puppies, and though under normal circumstances she would have liked to start with a puppy and watch it grow, what she needed was a dog that would be a guardian and defender of the house right now.

Three of the advertised dogs were full-grown, and calls to their present owners had made them seem possible choices. Around noon Claire had driven away in the Buick to look at the dogs, and none of the three of them was any good for her purpose. Feeling cranky and irritable at the waste of time and lack of success—and feeling worse because of the less than six hours' sleep she'd had—she got back to the house at two o'clock to be doubly irritated by the problem of the locked garage door.

The problem was, the doors could only be locked or unlocked from the outside. It made it very awkward. Sooner or later they'd have to install modern overhead doors, but in the meantime there didn't seem to be any way to have a lock on these doors that could be gotten at from both sides.

Now she unlocked and opened the doors, drove the Buick in, went back outside, closed and locked the doors again, and walked crunching across the stone driveway to the front door. Another key unlocked that, and she went in.

The only thing that bothered her about solitude was the absence of sound. She had brought the radio back to the kitchen when she'd gotten up this morning, and now she turned it on first thing, and started a pot of tea. In one of the Scandinavian countries they had recently introduced all-night radio for the first time, and the suicide rate dropped by an amazing percentage.

She ate a carton of vanilla yogurt while waiting for the tea. Dinner was the only true meal she ever ate, snacking the rest of the day on foods that were supposed to be good for dieters.

She poured a cup of tea to carry into the living room, and going down the hall past the open bedroom door she saw from the corner of her eye that a man was lying on the bed, on his back, his head propped up by a pillow; he was smiling dreamily through the window at the lake.

She went on another step before the image registered, and then stopped. A T-shaped iron bar of dread appeared within her back and shoulders, bowing her back, hunching her shoulders. The cup slopped tea on her thumb and fingers. She found she was blinking uncontrollably, and she made herself turn back, turn around and look at him again, in hopes that he wasn't really there.

She had gone beyond the doorway; it was necessary to take one dragging underwater

138

step back in the direction she'd come, and then she could see him. His shoes were off, showing black socks. He was wearing plaid bell-bottom slacks in shades of yellow and green, very dirty-looking. Some clothing was crumpled like laundry on the floor beside the bed, and above the trousers he was wearing only a gray-looking T-shirt, partly pulled out of the trousers. He wore a watch on his left wrist, with a very wide brown leather band; the wide band made her think of Roman slaves. He looked to be in his middle or late twenties and had long straight brown hair, very much like her own, only less well combed. He was slender, reasonably well built, but his face was fat, with puffy cheeks and protruding lips. She stood in the doorway, staring at him, and he made no move.

A sound behind her made her spin around, and she spilled more of the hot tea. She made a small high-pitched sound of terror in her throat, and looked at the other one, in the living-room doorway. He was wearing a fringed Davy Crockett jacket over a blue shirt streaked with gray as though Clorox had been dribbled over it. His black trousers were tucked into brown paratrooper's boots. He had a wild friz of hair, blondish-brown, a Caucasian equivalent of the hair-style called Afro, and he was smiling at her. He had the laughing eyes that go with sudden cruelty.

His voice was light, his manner flippant. He said, 'Don't bug Manny, he's trippin' out. Come on in here. What you got in the cup?'

She didn't move. She shook her head, not intending to.

He looked at her, and his expression became suddenly mean, though he still smiled. He said, 'You want pencils in the cup? I don't need you able to see, you know. Just so you can hear and talk, that's all I need.'

She didn't understand the specifics of the threat, but knew it was a threat and had no doubt he would do it, whatever it was. *I have to move*, she thought, *I have to do what he says*. She took one step forward, and the second was easier, and she walked toward him, the bones of her face standing out prominently around deep-set eyes.

He stepped to one side, grinning, bowing her into her living room. As she went by he lifted a hand, saying, 'What's in the cup?' He took it, tasted it, laughed in delight. 'Son of a bitch, it's *tea*! Isn't that cute? You take sugar in your tea, honey?'

Under the things he said, things moved that he didn't say. She shook her head. 'No, I don't.'

'That's too bad. Well, different strokes for different folks. Sit down on your sofa, honey, let's talk. Here, take your tea.'

She took the tea, went to the sofa, sat

140

down. The fireplace was directly in front of her, with yesterday's dead fire in it. The stones looked cold.

He didn't sit. He went over and stood at the corner of the fireplace, one foot up on the hearth, one elbow up on the mantelpiece with his hand dangling down, his other hand casually on his hip as he faced her. He said, 'We're looking for a friend of yours. Tell the truth, we thought we'd run into him here. When'll he be back?'

Cool, she thought. *Cunning*. She remembered what she'd said to Parker on the phone last night: 'I know how to be a little mouse.' Did she? She was blinking again, very badly, and was afraid that would betray her; he'd see the blinking and know she was lying. But it wouldn't stop, and she said, 'I don't know who you mean. I'm sorry, you have me frightened, but—' She raised her free hand and rubbed her eyelids hard with thumb and forefinger.

'Nothing to be frightened of,' he said, but he used a voice full of laughter and meanness. He said, 'We just want to see your friend, talk to him, maybe pick up a little something he's got for us.'

Her eyes hurt from the rubbing now, but the blinking went on. For an excuse to look away from him, and because she was afraid she would spill tea again, she half turned and put the cup on the end table, saying at the

141

same time, 'I live here alone.'

'A head like you? Don't do dumb lies, honey, we'll just make you pay for them.'

Now she did look at him, because what she had to say was technically true. 'I'm a widow,' she said. 'My husband was an airline pilot.'

His expression became uncertain; he said, 'What about Parker?'

'Mr. Parker? I only—'

'*Mister* Parker! God damn it, I don't like jokes!'

She was afraid he was going to rush at her and start punching and kicking. She cried, 'I just take messages! That's all, I swear that's all, I almost never see him, he never comes here!'

'You're a goddam liar. If he never comes here, how does he get the messages?'

'I call at a hotel in New York, and then he calls me back. Sometimes he comes out to pay me, but only two or three times a year.'

'You call a hotel in New York. You mean where he stays?'

'I don't know.'

'You don't talk to him?'

'No, I just leave a message with the desk.'

'The message you get, you leave at this hotel desk?'

'No. I call there, and I say I want to leave a message for Mr. Edward Latham. Then I just leave my name, and after a while he calls me back, and I tell him the message.'

He was frowning, and he said, 'That's awful damn complicated.'

'That's the way he wants to do it.'

Still standing in the same position, left leg up on hearth, right hand on hip, left elbow on mantelpiece, he gnawed a thumb-knuckle now and brooded. She watched him, watching him think about it and wondering whether the lie Parker had worked out for her would hold up or not. What if he decided to call the hotel?

'All right,' he said finally, and moved away from the fireplace. 'What's the hotel?'

'The Wilmington.'

'Move over.'

The phone was beside her. She got up and moved to the other end of the sofa, and he sat down and said, 'What's the number there?'

'I'll have to look it up.'

He frowned at her, with one hand resting on the phone. 'Look it up? You call this number all the time, you don't know it?'

'Not all the time. There aren't that many messages to pass on. And I'm terrible with numbers.'

'Terrible with numbers. I think you're lying, honey, and if it turns out you are, you'll go out screaming.' He turned his back on her, and picked up the phone, ready to dial.

In a small voice she said, 'You have to dial one first.'

He frowned at her again. 'What?'

'If you're calling New York, you have to—'

'Area code, I know.'

'No, before that. You have to dial one first. You see, this is just a little phone company out here, it isn't—'

'Shut up.' He said it flat and cold, and sat looking at her with totally blank eyes. All the mean comedy was gone from his face now. He said, 'I take very bad to frustration. I break my toys. You ought to be warned.'

She nodded, birdlike, afraid to speak.

He turned back to the phone and dialed one, and then the area code, and then a New York number. He waited, and his free hand tapped his knee. She looked at the hand, it was stubby-fingered and thick, the backs of the fingers covered with burns and scratches as though he'd been doing carpentry work without gloves. The nails were wide and stubby and dirty. The hand looked strong and humorless and mean.

'Hello, Information? Yes, hello, dear, Manhattan. Wilmington Hotel. Okay, dear, thanks a lot.' He broke the connection, started to dial again, stopped, said, 'Damn!' He started again; he'd forgotten to dial one, and he must have gotten the recorded announcement.

'Hello, Wilmington Hotel? Do you have a Mr. Latham registered there, Edward

Latham? Yeah, I'll wait.'

The stubby fingers tapped the rough cloth over his knee. His face was turned away from her, and the wildhaired back of his head told her nothing except that she should be afraid of him.

'Hello? Thursday? Hold one, there's somebody wants to leave a message for him.' He got to his feet, turning in a half-circle so he could extend the phone receiver over toward her. 'You want him to call you right away.'

She leaned leftward, taking the receiver, trying to think. What message would sound realistic to this man? What name should she use? The name on the mailbox, wouldn't that be safest? 'Hello?'

The voice of the disinterested desk clerk seventy miles away spoke in her ear: 'Yes?'

'I have a message for Mr.—Mr. Latham.'

'Yes?'

'Would he call Mrs. Willis as soon as possible.'

'Mrs. Willis was that?'

'That's right. He knows the number.'

'Very well. Call Mrs. Willis as soon as possible.'

'Yes, thank you.'

She started to get up to hang up the phone, but he took it from her hand and cradled it himself, then sat down on the sofa again beside her. 'Now we wait,' he said. The dancing movements were starting in his eyes again. He patted her knee. 'We wait and talk,' he said. 'We get acquainted.'

CHAPTER FIVE

He kept touching her, quick brief taps at her elbow, her knee, the back of her hand. It was sexual, the whole atmosphere of the situation was sexual, yet at the same time there was something remote and impersonal about his manner toward her. The thin humming aura of rape was in the air, but it was as though it would be rape without desire. A little later he would attack her, not because he wanted her in particular but simply because the situation seemed to him to call for it.

And in the meantime he sat beside her on the sofa and encouraged her to talk, about her parents, her upbringing, her dead husband, all sorts of things; and while she talked he kept touching her, small pointless taps at her elbow, her knee, her hand.

After a while she offered to make a fire, as an excuse to get up from the sofa, and he said sure, that was a fine idea. He didn't offer to help, but watched her crumple the paper and spread the kindling and carry in the logs from the porch, and all the time he watched her he had a happy smile on his face, as though she were doing something nice, especially for him.

She lit the fire, and he beamed at it and said, 'You know how to live. Away from the hassle, away from the whole thing.'

'Yes, it's nice.' She hoped he wouldn't notice that she'd chosen to stay on her feet, over by the fire, rather than sit down again on the sofa beside him.

'Yeah, this is what I want sometime. A house just like this. A nice fire, everything. Come sit down.'

She'd been holding the poker. Could she hit him with it? 'It's time for my pill,' she said. She put the poker down, leaning against the stone side of the fireplace.

'Pill? Birth control?'

'No, it's medicine. I'm supposed to take it every four hours.' She looked at her watch, and it was almost four o'clock. 'I'm due now.'

'Medicine?' He was frowning all over his face. 'What kind of medicine?'

'I don't know what it's called, it's a prescription.'

'What's it for?'

She allowed her nervousness to show, masking as embarrassment. 'I'd rather not talk about it.'

He got to his feet, his frown deeper. 'What the hell you talking about? Where is this medicine?'

'In the bathroom.'

147

'Let's go.'

She led the way down the hall toward the kitchen. The other one—Manny, this one had called him—was still lying in bed, facing the windows and the lake. He didn't seem to have moved in the last two hours.

There were two ways into the bathroom: a door from the bedroom and another from the kitchen. To avoid entering the room with Manny, Claire continued on down the hall and through the kitchen.

She remembered the bottle as being in the medicine chest; but what if she'd thrown it away? When she'd first come north from Florida to look for a house, a couple of months ago, she'd come down with some sort of flu, and a doctor in New York had given her a prescription for medicine. She tended to keep things like that around, just in case the same kind of illness should come back, but she wasn't entirely sure this bottle had survived the transition from the hotel in New York out here to the house.

Yes. She opened the mirrored door, and recognized it at once: a small clear plastic bottle with a white cap, up in a corner of the top shelf. The drugstore label on it looked nineteenth-century baroque. She took the bottle down and closed the door again, and he reached past her to pluck it out of her hand, saying, 'Let's see that.'

She stood beside the sink and he stood

between her and the doorway, frowning at the label on the bottle. She knew what it said: 'Mrs. Willis—one every four hours—Dr. Miller.'

He looked at her, looked at the bottle. 'It's a drugstore in New York,' he said.

'I didn't want anybody around here to know about it,' she said. It was a relief to be able to show how nervous she was, to use the true nervousness as a verification of the lie she was building.

'Every four hours,' he said, reading the label again. Then, 'Hey, this thing's two months old!'

The date. Down at the bottom of the label were the prescription number and the date; she'd forgotten about that. She stammered as she said, 'It's taking a while to cure it.'

'Cure it?' He frowned at her some more, and she could see him turning it over in his mind, not trusting it, not understanding what she might be up to and yet instinctively not trusting it. *I can't fool him*, she thought. *And because I tried to, he'll kill me*. She remembered what Parker had said when he'd called, about his friend having died of a painful illness, and all at once she was full of second thoughts. She should have taken Parker's advice and gone away from here. She shouldn't have tried this stunt with the medicine. It was going to end very, very badly, and it would be all her fault.

She was blinking again, forcing herself to meet his eyes, and she wished there was some way to make the blinking stop, it would betray her yet.

At last he looked down at the bottle again. 'Cure it,' he muttered, and snapped the lid off the bottle, and shook out three or four of the pills into the palm of his hand. They were smallish, round with beveled edges, robin's-egg blue. He shook the pills in his palm, watching them rock, and then lifted the plastic bottle and sniffed at the open top, like a wine connoisseur smelling the cork.

She watched him, tense and afraid. She knew what she wanted him to think, eventually, getting to the idea himself—but what was he thinking now? What was going on in his mind?

He lowered the bottle again, looked at the label, shook his head, eased all but one of the pills from his palm back into the bottle. Then he said, 'Fill that glass with water. No, just half full. Put it on the counter there.'

She put the glass on the glass counter under the medicine chest, and stepped back, and he came forward and dropped the pill into the water. It sank slowly, and they both watched it, and nothing happened.

This is comic, she thought. *This is hilarious. We're looking at a pill do nothing in a glass of water.*

She felt she was going to start laughing,

and dug her nails into her palms to keep it from happening. Because if she laughed he would be very angry and would do something to her. And because if she started to laugh she wouldn't be able to stop, and the laughing would become screams, and she wouldn't ever be able to make it stop.

The pill began very slowly to dissolve, like a fresh hairdo in a breeze, wispy lines of robin's-egg blue drifting upward.

He picked up the glass, shook it, smelled it, tasted the water very gingerly. Then he frowned, tossed the water into the sink, slapped the glass down on the counter again, went on holding the glass, stared grimly at it, and said, 'I want to know what those things are for. I don't want any more hacking around.'

'I was sick. It's a prescription for being sick.' She didn't want to say it to him, she wanted him to get to it himself; he would believe it more easily that way.

He turned his head slowly and looked at her, and for the second time she saw his eyes flat and blank and expressionless. 'I'm running out of patience, honey,' he said. 'What do you mean, sick?' Then his eyes narrowed and he said, 'Wait a minute. You mean the clap?'

Finally he'd come to it. But now there was another problem: the date on the bottle. She didn't know that much about gonorrhea, but she had the vague idea it didn't take two months to cure it. She said, tentatively, 'Well, something like that. That's why I didn't want to talk about it.'

'Something like that?'

'It takes longer. To be all right again.'

'Christ,' he said. He was disgusted, but her impression was that his disgust was caused by fastidiousness rather than disappointment; once again there was no feeling of any true sexual interest from him.

'That's why I went to New York,' she said. 'Because I didn't want anybody around here to know.'

'You got it around here,' he said. 'How the hell'd you manage that?'

She couldn't think of an answer right away, and just stood there helplessly.

He shook his head. 'Don't tell me your story, honey, I don't want to know. Here, take your pill.'

Her hand trembled as she took the bottle from him. She shook out one pill into her other palm, put the bottle away, refilled the glass, took the pill. He stood watching her, and when she put the glass back in its holder, he said, 'All right, come on.'

He had her walk ahead of him, and they left the bathroom and went through the kitchen and down the hall. He couldn't see her face now, and it could relax into whatever expression she wanted, and she was astonished to find that she was smiling.

Smiling? *I can handle him*, she thought. Managing the stunt with the illness had given her a sudden confidence, had given her back the self-assurance she'd had when she'd talked to Parker last night. These people were strong and mean and deadly and probably armed, but she was cleverer than they. The clever little mouse. She could play the dangerous game, after all, tiptoe between the lines of their understanding and never be seen.

And yet there was another feeling in her, too, stranger than the urge to smile and pat herself on the back. Coming along the hall, she could feel his disapproval as he walked behind her, and even though it was stupid and silly to think this way, she found herself hoping there'd be a chance later on to tell him the truth, that she didn't really have any kind of venereal disease, that it had only been to keep him from raping her that she had led him to believe it. No matter the situation, no matter the consequences she had escaped or the cleverness she had used, the fact of his disapproval and his belief in the reality of her illness hurt her pride, and she needed to believe she could rectify it later.

They were just entering the living room when the phone rang. At once he grabbed her elbow from behind and said, low-voiced in her ear, the words fast and urgent, 'You pick

153

it up after the third ring. Right after the third ring.'

'All right.' His fingers were painfully tight on her arm.

'And don't say anything stupid. Remember he's there and you're here.'

'I'll remember.'

He released her elbow and gave her a push into the living room. Without looking back, she knew he'd headed the other way; there was an extension phone in the bedroom, he'd listen there.

The phone rang for the second time as she hurried to the sofa. Was it going to be Parker? If not, would it be Handy McKay or somebody else who knew Parker lived here, and would they say something wrong? And if it was Parker, would *he* say something wrong?

In the silence between the second and third rings, she sat on the sofa and rubbed her knuckles into her eyes; the panicky blinking frightened and confused and distracted her.

The third ring. Seeing moons and planets around the periphery of her vision, after the hard rubbing, she rested one shaking hand on the phone and waited for the ring sound to stop. Her confidence had drained away again, all at once, as though it had never been. Her emotions were at the extremes, lunging between high and low, with no calmness at the middle.

Silence. She picked up the phone, said, 'Hello?'

Parker: 'Hello, it's me.'

She closed her eyes, squeezed them shut. That stopped the blinking, and for some reason made her more calm. 'Mr. Parker,' she said. 'Yes, I've been expecting you to call.'

There was no pause at all; he shifted into the new mode at once, saying, 'You have a message for me?'

'Yes.' The one now listening on the bedroom extension had coached her in this earlier, right after his call to the Hotel Wilmington. Conscious of him listening, she repeated what he'd told her to say: 'It isn't a message, exactly, it's a package. A Mr. Keegan came by and left it for you. He said you'd want to see it right away.'

'Mr. Keegan? What kind of package?'

'It's a small suitcase. I didn't open it. Can you come out tonight and pick it up?'

'Not tonight. I'm in Seattle right now, I won't be back East until Thursday.'

'Well, Mr. Keegan said this was important. He said it had to do with the concert, and you should get it right away.'

'Well, I'm tied up here in Seattle right now.' He was silent, thinking, and she tried to buzz her thought to him across the wire: *Get here now!* 'I could get there tomorrow night,' he said. 'Around eleven. That's the earliest I could make it.'

Down inside her closed eyes, she was

155

wondering, *Is he telling the truth?* But he wouldn't wait all that time, would he, knowing what the situation must be here now? He had to be just saying that, to lull the people he knew would be listening in. She said, 'Well, if that's the earliest—'

'Eleven tomorrow night.'

His voice is very dear to me, she thought, and was surprised at the tenderness she was feeling toward him. She usually considered both of them to be remote individuals, whose connection with one another was a convenience that fulfilled many needs, physical, emotional, psychic, but who were not sentimental about one another, any more than they were sentimental about themselves or anything else. And yet now she found herself reluctant to end the conversation with him, even though there was nothing more to be said, and it wasn't only because his voice was a symbolic lifeline to safety, though that was part of it, too. But the rest of it was tenderness, an outward flow of feeling toward him that the emotional onslaught of her situation had buffeted to the surface.

I have to hang up now, she thought. *A secretary only, a passer-on of messages.*

'Well, goodbye.'

'Tomorrow night,' he said. There was nothing in his voice, but that was all right. If she was doing things right, there was nothing in hers either.

'Yes, tomorrow night. Goodbye.'

'Goodbye.'

She kept her eyes squeezed shut, she continued to hold the phone to her face with both hands, and she listened to the click as he hung up, and then the furry silence of an open line. A second smaller click told her the listener in the bedroom had hung up.

It was time to get her report card, to find out whether or not this deception had earned a passing grade.

She opened her eyes at last, wearily, to put the phone down, and a round fat sunlike childish face was inches from hers, smiling broadly at her, the eyes bright and demented.

She screamed, and leaped backward along the sofa, throwing the phone at him without thinking. It missed his head and fell over his shoulder, the cord getting tangled in his right arm. He had been squatting in front of the sofa, grinning into her face, and now, with a comically blank surprised expression, he fell backward and bumped to a sitting position on the floor. He sat there, legs bent awkwardly in front of him, hands resting on knees, and gave a surprised laugh as he looked at her.

Her first terror ended quickly, and Claire looked more closely at him. This was Manny, who had been lying on the bed the last two hours. His face looked both guileless and mindless, as though he were a very happy moron. Could that be true, would the other one be traveling with somebody retarded?

Now the other one came into the living room, and said, 'What the hell's going on?'

Manny was picking the phone cord away from his arm as though it were imaginary and he were suffering from the d.t.'s. His voice happy and surprisingly light, he said, 'She threw the phone at me.'

'What was the scream about?'

'I'm sorry,' Claire said. The scream had rattled her, and she was very afraid again, as much so as when she'd first seen these two in her house. 'I didn't—I had my eyes closed, and I didn't know he was there.'

Manny had finally freed the phone, and now, hanging it up, he said, 'She looked just as nice. You wouldn't believe it, Jessup, she looked lovely. Like she was dead and all laid out.'

'Christ, Manny,' Jessup said, 'when do you come down?'

'Never, baby. I like it up here.' Manny grinned at Claire, and suddenly his expression became much more adult. Reaching out, he put the palm of one hand on the inside of her left knee, then slid his hand halfway up her thigh. 'You gonna come up with me?'

Jessup had come closer, and now his mouth moved in an expression of distaste. He said, 'Forget it, Manny. She's off limits.'

Manny pouted, like a sulky child, and looked around and up at Jessup. His hand stayed where it was, between her thighs. He said, 'How come? Where's the fun in that?'

'You better get your hand out of there, or you'll get clap of the fingernail.'

Manny frowned, like a stupid child laboriously learning multiplication tables, and looked again at Claire. 'A pretty lady like this? I don't believe it.'

'Go ahead, then.'

Claire waited, tensed, looking back at Manny, watching his mind deal with the problem. Jessup was intricate himself, the intricate could fool him. But Manny was direct.

And he asked her directly, 'You got something bad?'

Stupid; she felt embarrassed at lying to him. 'Yes,' she said, and had to look away. More and more stupid; tears were on her cheeks.

'Aw, hey,' His hand slid away, and Manny clambered up from the floor to sit beside her on the sofa and awkwardly pat her arm, to comfort her. 'Don't feel bad about it. That could happen to anybody.'

She didn't trust herself to answer him, the situation was too confused and unlikely. Her shoulders twitched and she shook her head and continued to face away from him.

'Listen,' he said. 'You wanna play Surrealism? You know how you play that?'

Now she did turn, and looked at him, and

159

found his childlike face twisted with sympathetic concern. 'No, I don't,' she said.

'You pick somebody famous,' he said. 'Like Humphrey Bogart or W. C. Fields or somebody. And then you say, if this person was a car he'd be such-and-such a kind of car. Or such-and-such a color. Or what season this person would be if they were a season. See, not what car would they *like*, what car would they *be*. Surrealism, see?'

'Yes, I think so.'

Manny turned his eager face. 'Jessup? You wanna play?'

'I'm hungry,' Jessup said. 'I want to get something to eat.'

'Why not have her get it?'

'I don't want her to touch my food. You want anything?'

'What for? You mean to eat? What for?'

Jessup shrugged. 'Keep an eye on her,' he said, and walked out of the room.

Manny turned back. 'Okay, I got somebody. Ask me a question. You know, like what car would I be or what color, or make up something.'

Claire tried to concentrate her mind. She was distracted by fear and uncertainty, and now she was supposed to think about a game. She rubbed her forehead and said, 'What car? I guess, that's what I want to know. What car would you be?'

'A Datsun,' he said promptly, and from the

160

way he grinned this was a person he had used in this game before. 'You tell me when you think you know who it is,' he said. 'Give me another question.'

Like she was dead and all laid out. That sentence of Manny's circled in her mind now every time she heard his voice. Was he a possible ally to be cultivated against Jessup, or was he the true danger?

'Come on,' he said, a happy impatient child. 'Come on.'

'What, uh—what color? What color would you be?'

CHAPTER SIX

When the doorbell rang, a little before nine, the three of them were eating dinner at the kitchen table. Jessup had insisted on preparing the meal himself, and then had insisted on Manny and Claire eating it with him, though neither of them had much appetite.

Claire found Manny both fascinating and terrifying. There was a temptation to react to him as though to a willful but charming child, but Manny was no child; he seemed, in fact, to be not human at all, and Claire found she was treating him finally like a charming but unpredictable animal, a pet that might or

161

might not be domesticated. As with an animal, the reasoning processes in Manny's head seemed both primitive and incomprehensible. And, as with an animal, Claire understood there would be no arguing against him if he should turn on her; as much argue with a leaping mountain lion. The strain of watching his volatile moods and trying to keep out in front of him was fraying her nerves, but distracting her from the larger problem of Jessup, who was after all the leader, the man with the reins of the situation in his hands.

Whatever Manny was high on—and it was clear he'd been taking some sort of drug—the peak had apparently passed during his time in the bedroom, leaving him now in a pleasant cloudy afterglow, his mind turning slowly and coming up with strange materials from the bottom of his skull. The game of Surrealism had been full of a kind of morbid beauty, Manny's images sometimes being very odd and personal and irrational, but frequently they contained touches of poetry and at times were amazingly indicative of the person he had in mind.

But always dead people. They had taken turns asking the questions, and when Claire had chosen a living woman senator, it had taken Manny a long time to guess who she meant, and then he was angry and upset. 'No fair, she's still alive!'

'You didn't tell me we were—'

'You can't use live people! They don't have any *aura*!'

So they had remembered only dead people after that.

Jessup had refused to join in the game. Now that his larger game, whatever it was, had moved into a phase of waiting—he expected to have to wait thirty-one hours from Parker's phone call to Parker's appearance here—Jessup was surly and uncommunicative. The sparks and flashes of light were deep in his eyes, but they showed as irascibility and bad temper now.

Somehow the meal he'd prepared reflected his mood. It was vaguely Mexican, full of tomatoes and peppers, very hot, and lay in an unappetizing mass on the plate. But Jessup watched the two of them with narrowed eyes, demanding that they eat, and they both ate, Manny making a game out of this too, joking with Jessup about the meal looking like dead people's stomachs, while Claire mechanically moved the fork from plate to mouth, plate to mouth.

The doorbell both shocked and relieved her; she had no idea who it could be or what it could mean, but it made it possible, at least for the moment, to stop eating. She put the fork down at once, and looked across the table at Jessup.

Jessup was looking twice as irritable as

before. He said, low-voiced, 'Who is it?'

'I don't know.'

'You don't expect anybody?'

'No. Really.'

'If you're trying something—'

'I'm not,' she insisted. 'Really.' She felt she was going to cry; to get away with so many lies, and then to have him about to do something to her for something she hadn't done—it wasn't fair.

Jessup got to his feet. 'We'll be close enough to hear,' he said. 'Manny, come over here with me.'

The two of them went into the front left corner of the kitchen, where they would be out of sight of anyone outside the doorway. 'Answer it,' Jessup said. 'If it's somebody that has to come, we're friends, we dropped in for a Mex dinner.'

Claire went to the door and opened it. One of the few things that had bothered her about this house when she'd first seen it was the lack of an entrance foyer, the main door opening from the driveway directly into the kitchen. She wondered now if that would have made any difference, if a foyer or entranceway would have given her a few seconds in which to whisper a warning to whoever was at the door.

There was no way to tell, and in any case there was nothing but the door. She opened it and a youngish man was standing there, his

164

hair moderately long in what used to be called a pageboy style. He was wearing a sheepskin jacket, his hands were in the jacket pockets, and he was smiling. 'Hello,' he said. 'My name is Morris. I'm looking for a fellow called Parker.'

Morris. She remembered the name from Parker's description of the robbery; this was the man who'd stood on watch on the roof. 'Mr. Parker isn't here,' she said, suddenly very nervous, wondering how much Parker had told Morris, wondering if Morris would expose her lies now.

And at the same time she was speaking, she heard Jessup, low-voiced, saying from the corner, 'Invite him in.'

'Won't you come in, Mr. Morris?'

'Well, it's Parker I'm looking for. He isn't here?'

'Not right now. Come in, let's not stand in the doorway.'

'Thanks.' Morris came through the doorway, still smiling, saying, 'You expect him back—'

Jessup and Manny were walking forward, both of them smiling. 'Hi,' Jessup said. 'I'm Jessup. We just stopped in for some Mex dinner.'

Morris kept the smile on his face, but his eyes were suddenly watchful, and his hands came out of his jacket pockets. 'Jessup? You a friend of Parker's?'

165

'We're more friends of Mrs. Willis here,' Jessup said.

Morris looked at Claire, who strained to be natural in her appearance and the sound of her voice, saying, 'That's right, they're old friends of mine. They knew I was all alone here, so they dropped in. That's Manny.'

Manny grinned happily and said, 'Hi, baby. Did you say your name was Morris?'

'That's right.'

Manny giggled, and poked Jessup. 'That's a coincidence, ain't it?'

'That's right,' Jessup said, though he didn't sound happy about Manny's saying it. He explained to Morris, 'We were looking for a guy by that name a while ago. We were supposed to do a job with him, but we couldn't find him. Down in Oklahoma, around there.'

'In Oklahoma.' Morris turned his head and said to Claire, 'You expect Parker back soon?'

'Well, Mr. Parker doesn't *live* here,' she said. If he knew the truth, she hoped he was fast enough to adjust. He looked as though he probably was. 'But I do expect to see him—'

'Later tonight,' Jessup said. 'In fact, we figured we might play a little cards later on, when he got here.'

'Or Surrealism,' Manny said. To Morris he said, 'You ever play Surrealism?'

'Once.'

'Really? Isn't it great? This lady here is

166

great at it, ain't you?'

'Not as good as you are,' Claire said. She even managed a smile.

Jessup said, 'Hey, why don't we eat? Morris, you hungry? You like Mex?'

'I could eat.'

'You all sit down,' Claire said. 'I'll set the place.'

She tried to maneuver herself into a position where neither Jessup nor Manny could see her face, so she could signal Morris somehow, but Jessup kept turning around in his chair, watching her, asking brightly if he could help. She saw that Morris watched Jessup and Manny with slightly narrowed eyes, suspicious in a small way, but not at all sure something was wrong.

Food was dished out for Morris, and then they all sat down again, Claire facing Morris, Jessup to her left, Manny to her right.

Jessup said, 'How come you're looking for Parker? Business?'

'In a way,' Morris said.

Jessup gave Claire a brief noncommittal glance, then said to Morris, 'I guess everybody knows to come here if they want to see Parker.'

'Not exactly,' Morris said. 'I got the address from a friend.'

'A friend?'

'A fellow named Keegan.' Morris looked

around pleasantly. 'Any of you people know him?'

Claire recognized the name as the man Parker had gone to see, the one who had gotten the phone number here from Handy McKay. The one who had died a painful death.

Jessup was saying, 'Keegan? Keegan? I don't think so.'

Manny said, 'I knew a Keeler once.'

Jessup said, 'Where's this guy Keegan live?'

'He doesn't,' Morris said. 'He's dead. Say, this stuff is pretty good.' Meaning the plate of food in front of him.

Jessup had just taken a big second helping for himself. 'Yeah, it is,' he said. 'One of my favorites. You say this guy Keegan is dead?'

'Well, I'll tell you what the situation is,' Morris said, 'and maybe you might be able to help me out. See, Keegan and Parker and another fellow and I were together last week, but then we went our separate ways. Then I heard from a friend of mine that Keegan had been asking around for me, trying to find me. So I knew where he was, so I went to see him. And damn if he wasn't dead. Somebody had nailed him to a wall.'

The phrase was so absurd that it skimmed the surface of Claire's mind at first, and it was only when Jessup repeated it, in tones of shock, that she really heard what had been said: 'Nailed him to a wall!'

'It seemed like a hell of a thing to do,' Morris said. 'I always thought Keegan was kind of grumpy myself, but I think that was probably more than he deserved.'

Manny said, 'Gee. Nailed him to a wall. How about that?' He wasn't as good an actor as Jessup, who gave him a hard look to shut him up.

'I searched the place,' Morris said. 'Somebody else had searched it, but I did anyway, and I found Parker's name on a sheet of paper with a phone number in New Jersey. So I took it along, and I went looking for a fellow named Berridge.'

Jessup said, 'Berridge? Who's he?'

'He's somebody else that's dead,' Morris said, and looked at Claire. 'I hope you don't know any of these people, Mrs. Willis. I'm sorry to be talking about death so much at your table.'

'No, that's all right,' she said, stumbling. 'I mean, I don't know them.' She didn't know Berridge.

Morris said, 'Berridge is an old man who was going to work with Parker and Keegan and that other fellow and me, but he decided he was too old, and then he got killed. I figured maybe, since Berridge had been the first one killed, maybe somebody that knew Berridge would know what was going on. So I went and talked to some people who knew Berridge, and I found out Berridge had been

169

having a lot of trouble with a grandson of his. The grandson had been hustling him for money. Apparently he's an acidhead of some kind.'

The air in the room had suddenly changed. No one was eating, or even pretending to eat. Morris was talking calmly, as though there were no tension in the air at all, but Claire could see in his cheekbones, in the way he moved his eyes, that he too was tense.

She shifted her gaze without turning her head—she was almost afraid to turn her head—and saw Manny looking sullenly at Morris, his head down like a bull when frustration is about to make it charge.

Jessup, his voice flat, said, 'You think this grandson had something to do with what happened to Berridge and Keegan?'

Morris said, 'I think Berridge had promised the grandson money out of this work he was going to do with the rest of us. But then the old man lost his nerve or his wind or something, and the grandson was stuck. So I think the grandson decided to take the money away from the other guys, from me and Parker and Keegan and the other fellow. And I think Berridge was going to warn us about it, and the grandson killed him. But Berridge had told the grandson where we were going to be at one certain point, so the grandson hung around until we left that place, and then picked one of us to follow, and it happened to be Keegan.'

Jessup said, 'To rob him, you mean.'

'That's right. And to find out from him how to reach the rest of us. What I don't understand is the torture, though.'

Claire said, 'Torture?' She hadn't known she was going to say anything at all, and the sound of the word in her own voice startled and frightened her. Vague images of torture—fire, pinching things, whips, electricity—flickered like bits of a silent movie in her mind.

Morris looked at her. 'I'm sorry, Mrs. Willis. I won't describe it. But what I don't understand is why it was done.'

Jessup said, 'Maybe this fellow Keegan wanted to keep some of the money for himself. Maybe he wouldn't tell the grandson where it all was, just one little part of it.'

Morris shook his head. 'Keegan wasn't crazy. He'd rather be alive and poor than dead and rich. Besides, there wasn't that much money to give over.'

Jessup said, 'How much?'

'I suppose Keegan would have gotten home with about sixteen thousand,' Morris said.

Manny made a sudden startled sound, and Jessup said, quickly, 'That little? For the kind of thing he was doing?'

'When you figure it was one night's ticket receipts, and it was split four ways, and the financing had to come out of it, there wasn't that much left.' Morris looked appraisingly at Jessup, and said, 'Do you suppose that's what happened? Do you suppose Keegan gave the sixteen thousand to the grandson and he wouldn't believe that was all of it? Do you suppose they tortured Keegan to death trying to get him to give them something he didn't have?'

Claire said, 'That's awful. He wouldn't have any way to make them stop.'

'He could die,' Jessup said. Though he was answering Claire, he kept looking at Morris. He said, 'So what now?'

'I came here,' Morris said. 'The phone number got me the address. I figured Parker ought to know what was going on, and maybe I'd run into the grandson around here someplace.'

'Well, he hasn't showed up yet,' Jessup said. 'Maybe because Parker isn't here, or because he saw Mrs. Willis had friends with her.'

'To protect her,' Manny said. The words had a curious leaden quality to them, as though he didn't understand English but was reading a prepared speech written down phonetically.

Jessup said, 'What's the grandson's name?'

'Berridge, like his grandfather.' Morris grinned at him and said, 'Your name's Jessup.'

'That's right.'

Morris turned his head and looked at Manny. 'And your name's Manny. That's your first name, isn't it?'

What happened next was very fast and very confusing. Morris' hands moved and there was a quick glimpse of a gun coming out from under the sheepskin jacket, but at the same time Jessup flung his plate of food into Morris' face, and Manny grabbed up the steak knife they'd been cutting the Italian bread with and lunged forward to jab it into Morris' left side just above his belt.

Then everyone was standing, and Morris' and Claire's chairs had tipped over backward. The gun was no longer in Morris' hand, which now was clutched around the wooden handle of the steak knife; his other hand was wiping frantically at the food smeared on his face, trying to get it out of his eyes.

Claire was backing away, her mouth open wide, grimacing with the pressure of trying not to scream. Jessup had gone down on one knee for the gun, but Manny had grabbed up his fork and was poking it at the food on Morris' face and then into his own mouth, at Morris' face and into his mouth, fast hard movements, and at the same time laughing and shouting, 'Look! I'm eating! Look at this! I'm eating!' Morris was trying to keep away from the fork, and not fall over the chair lying down behind him, and get the food—it must be stinging him—out of his eyes, and do

173

something about the knife in his side, and stay alive, and none of it was going to happen.

Jessup came up with the gun, and Morris went crashing backward over the chair, and Manny yelled with laughter and lunged after him, and Claire turned and ran full-tilt for the bedroom.

CHAPTER SEVEN

'Come out of there, honey,' Jessup called, and tapped on the bedroom door.

The last five minutes had been full of pointless frantic activity. She'd run in here and locked the door and pulled the dresser over in front of it to block it. And then there was the door to the bathroom—they could get into the bathroom from the kitchen, and then through this other door into here—and she jammed a chair-back under the door handle of that. And there was the glass door to the porch and the outside. And flanking it were windows.

Parker had been right. There was no way to lock yourself safely into this house. Too many doors, too many windows.

And now, too late, she realized she should have left the house at once, when she'd run in here. She should have kept on going, through the bedroom and out the door to the porch and across the yard and away from here.

There'd been a scream, just one, very hoarse, less than a minute after she'd come in here, while she was still barricading the first door, but there hadn't been another sound since then. Where were they now, what were they doing?

It was too late to run now. She'd been mindless and frantic when she'd run into this room, and because of that she'd thrown away her chance, while they were both concerned with Morris.

But why hadn't they come after her? She turned and stared hard at the windows, half-expecting to see Manny's moon face grinning at her there, but the porch was empty.

Was there still time? Or were they playing cat and mouse with her, making believe they weren't thinking about her, waiting for her to make the jump and try to get away? That would be like them, that would be their style. Let her think she still had a chance, and then do something really awful to her.

Once before, since the start of her involvement with Parker, people from his world had intruded into hers, bringing discomfort and danger with them, but that time the people involved had been rational and businesslike. They'd wanted Parker to do something, he hadn't wanted to do it, they'd tried to use her for leverage against him. She had been afraid, but not the way she was afraid now, because that time she'd been dealing with sane human beings who wouldn't do anything pointless. But Jessup and Manny weren't sane, and they were barely human beings. It was as she'd thought before, like having a mountain lion loose in the house; no way to talk to him, no way to guess what he'll do next, no way to reason with or about him at all.

She stood blinking and immobile in the middle of the bedroom, the two doors barricaded, the third door and the windows still unblocked, and for a minute she was incapable of any kind of movement at all. And then Jessup called, and tapped on the hall door, and she took a fast aimless step to nowhere.

The porch door. Out, or block it? How barricade a glass door? How barricade the windows flanking it?

Jessup, sounding bored and irritable, called a second time, 'Don't make it tough on yourself, honey. Open the door and come out.'

What if she were to hide? What if she hid, and led them to believe she already *had* escaped from the house?

But where? Where, in this small and simple bedroom? The closet, no good. Behind the drapes, no good. Under the bed, no good.

Under the bed.

The doorknob rattled. Jessup called, 'I hate physical labor, bitch! You better open this door!'

Was it still there? She dropped to her knees and looked wildly under the bed, and the rifle was lying there where she'd left it, slender, long. She started to reach for it, and then suddenly became aware of the light in the room and the darkness outside, and how this room was now like a stage set. And was there an audience, outside the windows, in the darkness on the porch?

To have Jessup hammer and threaten at the hall door, and Manny waiting and grinning outside on the porch, hoping she would try to make a run for it—that was their style.

She left the rifle where it was, and got again to her feet. She moved awkwardly now, self-consciously, convinced that eyes were watching her.

The night-table lamp on her side of the bed was the only source of light. She moved to it, cumbersome, uneasy, blinking, and bent suddenly to switch it off. In the new darkness she dropped to the floor again, felt along the bed, reached her hand underneath and slapped at the floor till she felt the cold metal of the rifle barrel. And all the time wincing from the expected sound of breaking glass, sure that Manny would crash into the room now from the porch.

But nothing happened. She pulled the rifle

out, sat up, and leaned her back against the side of the bed. She sat cross-legged, tailor fashion, with the rifle across her lap; the barricaded hall door was to her left, the vulnerable porch door to her right.

Nothing happened.

Was that voices, was that movement?

Jessup's voice, low and threatening, sounded from against the blocked door: 'Manny says you've turned out the light. You goin' to bed now? But you got to finish your dinner.'

So she'd been right. Manny had been watching the porch door, that was the only way he could know the light had been turned off.

She thought of shouting to them that she was armed, that they should go away, but she was afraid that would simply make them meaner and more difficult to deal with. It was the mountain lion again; you can't scare off a mountain lion by telling him you have a gun.

Jessup called, 'Honey, you can come out now and everything'll be okay, no trouble at all. But you stay in there and you'll be sorry.'

It was such a temptation to believe him. It would be so much easier that way, to hide the rifle again under the bed, pull the dresser away from the door, and just walk out there. If she could believe him.

She didn't move.

Nothing happened then for a long while.

She continued to sit there, straining to hear a sound that would tell her what they were doing, what they were planning to do.

Where was Parker? Five hours since he'd called.

Noises. Bumping and thumping in the living room, Manny and Jessup saying things to one another. She couldn't make out the words, but it sounded as though they were doing some sort of work together and were giving one another instructions and comments.

Her eyes had grown more used to the darkness. It was an overcast night, with intermittent starshine; the rectangles of door and windows were paler blurs in the darkness, and at intervals she could make out the light-reflecting restless water of the lake.

The thumping noises were coming closer, moving now across the porch from the direction of the living-room door. Were they bringing something heavy to batter their way through this door? *I can't faint*, she told herself, her arms were trembling, her stomach was light and queasy, and the blinking was back again, worse than ever.

What were they *doing*? Vaguely she saw movement outside, on the porch. They were out there, or one of them was out there.

Should she shoot at them through the glass? But they were so vaguely seen, and it was probably only one of them anyway, and

179

the chances were she wouldn't hit them at all, not under these conditions. And afterward they would know she had a gun.

Dragging sounds, rustling movements, half-seen busyness out there on the porch. And then nothing. There still seemed to be someone or something there, a vague shape bulky outside the glass door, but she couldn't make out what it was.

Turn on the light? But that would illuminate her much more than it.

There were porch lights, two of them, operated by a pair of switches, one beside the door in here and one beside the door in the living room. Either switch operated both lights. She could crawl over to the door—standing up and walking was beyond her now—and reach up and turn on the porch lights, and then she would know what it was out there. But did she really want to know?

She shifted position, turning half-around on the floor so as to put her left side toward the porch. She raised the rifle and pointed it at the bulky thing beyond the door.

Nothing happened. She waited, and nothing happened.

And then the porch lights came on, suddenly, unexpectedly, and she screamed at what was outside the door, looking in at her.

Morris. Dead and naked and cut all over his body and tied upright in a kitchen chair. Just sitting there, with his arms hanging

180

down at his sides, his head dangling to the right, his eyes looking at her.

She emptied the rifle into him, and the laughing kept on anyway, and she was squeezing the trigger to make click sounds against emptiness when Jessup and Manny punched their way in through the bathroom door.

PART FOUR

CHAPTER ONE

The plane circled Newark for fifteen minutes, and had been late getting there in any event. It was nearly eight o'clock before they landed and the passengers could get off.

At night, Newark Airport looks like Newark: underilluminated, squat, dirty. The terminal building seemed to be full of short people speaking Spanish, all of them excited about one thing or another. Parker went through them like a panther through geese, and trotted across the blacktop street out front to the parking lot and the Pontiac.

He had major highway to drive on most of the way, with country blacktop for only the last ten miles or so. He drove by the turnoff to the road that circled the lake, knowing that just over a mile farther on, the other end of the same road came around to intersect with the one he was on.

There'd been a lot of traffic coming the other way, eastbound, weekenders on their way back to the city, and a car was waiting to come out at the second turnoff. Parker steered around it, and met two others coming out while he drove in. He would have preferred a week night, when there'd be a lot less activity around the lake.

He picked a likely-looking house on the

lake side of the road, one that showed no lights or any sign of recent activity, but which didn't have its windows boarded up for the winter. He left the Pontiac in the driveway, looked through one of the windows in the garage door, and saw a fairly large outboard motorboat in there, on a wheeled carrier. So the owner hadn't started coming up yet this year at all, or the boat would be in the water and room would have been left in the garage for their car.

Parker walked around the side of the house and down the slope of weedy lawn at the back to the water's edge, and looked out across the lake. There were maybe fifteen houses showing light over there; one of them would be Claire's. He was too far away now to make out anything but light and darkness.

The house here was built on land that sloped pretty steeply down toward the water, so that what was the first floor on the road side was a good eight feet above the ground back here, held up by a series of metal posts. Part of the underneath section had been closed off to form a sort of workshop, and the rest was left open and used for storage of various things: a lawnmower, jerry cans, an oildrum-and-wood-platform float, and two aluminum rowboats.

Parker wrestled one of the rowboats out of the storage space, turned it right side up, and dragged it down to the water's edge. Then he went back and found several wooden oars, their green paint flaking off, leaning against the rear of the storage space. He brought them down to the rowboat, fit them into the oarlocks, and pushed the boat into the water.

It was a cloudy night, with occasional spaces of starry sky but no moon. Parker set off in the rowboat, and twenty feet from shore he could no longer clearly make out the house he'd started from.

It was a cool evening, but the rowing was warm work. The boat moved well enough so long as he kept at the oars, but it never built up any momentum; the instant he would stop to rest, the boat would sag to a halt in the water.

Out in the middle, he stopped for a minute to study the far shore, trying to figure out which house was Claire's. But it still wasn't possible, the lights were anonymous, not giving a clear enough indication of the shape of any of the buildings, and he was still much too far away to make out the rooms inside any of those lit windows.

He saw that his tendency while rowing was to veer slightly to the left, probably because his right arm was the stronger. When he started again now, he picked one of the lights back on the shore he'd left, and tried to keep that light on a direct line with the rear of the rowboat. When he looked over his shoulder at the shore he was approaching, it seemed to be

187

working; so far as he could tell he was now traveling in a straight line.

Glimpses of the main road could be seen far away to the left, beyond the end of the lake; a steady stream of headlights made a broken white line marking the route. Parker knew approximately how far in from that road Claire's house stood, and there were four or five houses showing light in the right area. He was aiming for the one farthest to the left, and when he got close enough to make out details he would turn and parallel the shore until he got to the right house.

The first one wasn't it. It had no boathouse, and the porch was a different shape.

Sound travels across the water. There were two young boys fishing off a wooden dock at the second house, and though he was well out from shore he could hear every word they said to one another. They were arguing, quietly and dispassionately, about which one of them had lost a missing lure. Parker rowed past, out beyond the reach of the light-spill from the house behind the boys, and at one point the right oarlock made a metallic creaking sound, not very loud. At once the boys stopped talking, and he could see their silhouettes as they gazed out in this direction. He kept rowing, now making no sound other than the dip of oar blades in and out of the water.

One of the boys said, 'There's somebody out there in a rowboat.'

'He'll hear you.'

'That's all right. Maybe he's got that Big Red, since you don't have it.' And they went back to their reasonable bickering about the lure.

There were five dark houses before the next lit one. Out in the middle of the lake there'd been a little breeze-chop making wavelets that had slowed the boat some, but in closer to shore the water was almost completely flat, with only a slight ripple from the breeze, and the boat cut through it faster and more smoothly.

He recognized the boathouse first, even though this was the only time he'd seen it from this direction. But he knew it was the right house before he could see it clearly, and he rowed more cautiously, shipping the oars at last and letting the boat drift the short distance in to the boathouse.

The living room was lit, the bedroom was dark. He could see no one through the living-room windows. Light-spill on the side of the house told him the kitchen lights were on.

He took out the automatic from under his arm and held it in his right hand while with his left he maneuvered the boat around the front of the boathouse and along the wooden dock on the side. The shore was finished with a concrete patio, so he kept the boat from drifting all the way in; he didn't want the clatter of aluminum on concrete.

The boat had its own frayed rope, one end tied to a ring at the prow. There were several rings set at intervals along the outer edge of the dock, and Parker put the automatic down on the dock while he made the boat fast. Then he picked up the gun again and stepped up cautiously onto the dock.

Was that movement on the porch? He stood on the dock, against the boathouse's side wall, and watched and waited. Nothing happened, and then a figure—two figures—moved past the lit windows from left to right. The door between the living room and the porch opened and closed.

Parker waited. Nothing else happened. He had the vague impression of people moving in the living room, but the angle was wrong to make out what they were doing.

He moved out away from the boathouse wall and came cautiously in off the dock, moving at an angle that would take him eventually to the lightless bedroom. The tall skinny trees spaced around the lawn obscured his view of the house slightly without giving him any cover. He moved up through them, eyes scanning the house, automatic ready in his right hand.

The porch lights snapped on, and a second later the night erupted in rifle shots and screaming and the clatter of breaking glass. There was something on the porch in front of the bedroom door, Parker couldn't see what; he crouched low and ran forward, now aiming more to the right, toward the living room.

Claire had said she'd bought a rifle.

The noise ended as abruptly as it had started: first the scream, then the glass, and finally the flurry of shots. None of the rifle fire seemed to have been aimed in Parker's direction.

In the new silence, Parker moved along the edge of the screened-in porch toward the stoop and the screen door. Looking back to his left, he could see now what was in front of the bedroom door: a chair, facing the bedroom, with somebody sitting in it. Tied to it. Unconscious, or dead. The chair was turned away so that Parker couldn't see who it was or anything else about him.

The porch lights were a nuisance, but the screaming had given him a greater sense of urgency. He went up the stoop, crouching, looking every way at once, and another scream sounded from the bedroom; louder, more shrill and hopeless than before.

Parker pushed at the screen door and the latch was on. He kicked the sole of his foot against the wood of the door just above the knob, and the door popped wide open, as though in invitation. He jumped through, looked to the right and ran left, toward the bedroom. He stopped behind the chair, looked over the shoulder of the thing sitting in it, and saw Claire sitting in the middle of the floor, clutching a rifle in both hands. Behind her, the hall door was barricaded with the dresser. To the left, the bathroom door had been locked, but had now been broken open, and two shaggy-looking men were standing just inside the doorway. One of them, moon-faced and grinning, started toward Claire as though he were a child and she a piece of candy. The other one, more hawklike, stood back with the small smile of the spectator on his mouth.

Parker lifted the hand with the automatic in it. The hawklike one saw the movement, saw him standing there, and yelled, 'Manny! Back!'

Manny? Parker fired at him, but Manny was already turning and the bullet didn't hit him right; it caught him in the upper left arm and knocked him sprawling on his face on the floor in front of the bed.

Claire had flung the rifle away and lunged for the side of the bed, to press herself against the floor there.

The hawklike one had suddenly developed a gun. He fired twice, both bullets going wide, and shouted, 'Manny, for Christ's sake, get up!'

It was tough, from outside the room, to get a good shot at either of them. Having already wounded Manny, Parker tried for the other one, but the shot missed, and after it the guy ducked back through the doorway. And Manny had gotten his feet under him; in a scrabbling lunge, half-run and half-crawl, he catapulted himself across the open space and through the bathroom door and out of sight.

Parker knocked over the chair with the dead man in it, to get it out of his way. The glass door was locked; he reached through the broken part and unlocked it, then slid it open and stepped inside.

Claire was still cowering on the floor beside the bed. Parker left her there for now, and followed the two men.

He was slowed down because he couldn't go through any doorway or around any corner without first being sure they weren't waiting for him on the other side. But when he got to the kitchen he saw the outside door standing open, and heard the roar of a car starting up. The kitchen was a mess, chairs overturned and slop everywhere; he saw it without thinking about it yet, and ran to the front door.

The light switch on the wall beside the door turned on two outside lights, an ornamental fixture beside the door and a floodlight mounted over the garage doors. Parker hit that switch on the way by, and where there had been darkness outside the doorway there was now the gravel driveway and two cars: a white Plymouth and a dark blue Corvette. They had been parked side by side in front of the door, the 'Vette nearest the house, and it was the 'Vette that was now in motion, backing fast and curving to put its taillights against the garage doors and point its nose down the driveway toward the road.

Parker got one shot at it while it was broadside to him over there, the driver shifting out of reverse. He didn't bother to try for the driver, who was in any case crouched low in the seat and was a chancy target in this light. He shot the left front tire, and when the 'Vette surged forward, spraying gravel back onto the garage doors, Parker fired a second time and put out the left rear tire. The 'Vette slued badly, but kept moving. Parker ran forward three strides, turned sideways to the fleeing car, and tried to plant a bullet in the right rear tire, but apparently missed. As the 'Vette was grinding through the turn onto the road, swaying and bumping badly with both left tires out, Parker made a try for the gas tank, firing two shots into the car's body. Then it was out of range of the floodlight, though for a few seconds longer he could still hear it.

He half-turned and ran to the garage to get out Claire's Buick, but there were padlocks on the doors that hadn't been there thirty-six hours ago.

The Plymouth? He went to it and opened it

and the keys weren't in the ignition. He hadn't really expected them to be, but it was worth a try.

So they'd made it. For now.

Parker went back into the house, shutting the door behind himself and switching off the lights again. He kept the automatic in his hand and walked back through the bathroom into the bedroom.

Claire was sitting on the bed. She looked weary, but not hysterical. She lifted her head when he walked into the room, and said, 'They got away?'

'For now. How are you?'

'A nervous wreck. I'm glad you got here.'

He went over and stood in front of her and put a hand on her shoulder. 'I came as fast as I could.'

'I know you did.' She patted his hand. 'It was very scary, waiting. I'm going to have nightmares for a while.'

'Can you tell me about them? Can you talk yet?'

'Not till you get rid of that.' She moved her head slightly, without turning it, the gesture indicating the porch.

He glanced that way and saw the overturned chair with the body tied to it. He still hadn't seen the face, still knew only that it was male and naked and dead and messy. He said, 'Was that one of them?' Thinking

195

there might have been a falling-out among them.

But she shook her head. She was looking straight ahead, at his belt buckle, as though she had to have a very tight rein on herself right now. She said, 'Morris. From the robbery.'

'Morris? He came here with them?'

'I'll tell you about it,' she said, and now there was more vibrato in her voice, more trembling. 'But first you have to get rid of it. You have to.'

'All right,' he said. 'I'll get rid of it.'

CHAPTER TWO

It was simplest, despite the chill in the air, to do the job naked. It was going to be messy, and this way there'd be no clothing to be cleaned afterward.

But first there were preparations to be made. Parker found Morris' clothes in the kitchen, ripped and torn and bloodied and strewn around the floor. He searched them for the keys to the white Plymouth outside, then bundled them up and carried them around the outside of the house to leave them temporarily with the body. He took the long way so as not to carry the bundle past Claire, and saw through the shattered glass door that she was no longer in the bedroom. He could hear water running in the tub.

He drove the Plymouth around the lake, taking the opposite direction from that of the Corvette, which meant he would follow the loop of road around the lake without coming out on the main road, with all its citybound traffic.

He knew it was a risk, leaving the house again, but it was one he had to take. The two in the Corvette wouldn't get very far with a pair of tires gone, so they'd still be in the neighborhood for a while, but it was unlikely they'd choose to come back to Claire's house, knowing it was now occupied by a man with a gun.

He passed the house where he'd borrowed the rowboat; his Pontiac still sat quietly in the driveway. And about half a dozen houses beyond that, where he had noticed on the way in a family loading their car, there was now no car, and the house was in darkness. Parker turned the Plymouth in at that driveway, left it, and went around to the boathouse, which was locked. Wood near water doesn't last long; it took two kicks to spring the screws loose holding the hasp, and the door sagged open.

The boat inside was a fiberglass outboard with a forty-horsepower Johnson motor. Parker raised the overhead door at the lake end of the boathouse, untied the motorboat from its three moorings; stepped in, and started the motor. He backed out through the wide doorway, turned the boat around, and headed at open throttle across the lake.

Fewer houses were lit now, and with the porch lights still glowing, it was easier to recognize Claire's place. Parker eased the motorboat in toward shore, nestled it between the rowboat and the concrete, and tied it to another of the rings along the edge of the dock.

Claire was in the tub. She looked up when he came in, and her face seemed simultaneously drawn and puffy, a contradiction that made her look almost as though she'd been partying too much for several nights in a row. She said, 'Is it gone yet?'

'Soon. You still want to stay here?'

She looked wary. 'Why?'

'I shot out their tires, they'll still be around the lake someplace. After I'm done here I'll go look for them, but in the meantime they might come back. While I'm gone.'

'They won't come back.' She sounded grim, but sure of herself.

'I don't think so either. But they might. I wounded one of them.'

'That's why they won't come back. They're cowards, you'll see. They'll hide in a hole someplace.'

'I think so, too. But just in case.'

'I'm too tired to go anywhere,' she said.

'Too tired and too scared and too nervous. You were right before, I should have gone to a hotel. But now I can't, I can't do anything.'

'I'll be as fast as I can.'

His first move was to switch off the bedroom and porch lights, and then to strip down. He stuffed his clothing in a pillowcase and took it down across the backyard and put it on the seat of the motorboat. Then he went back up to the darkened porch and put the chair back up on its legs and dragged it backward over to the door.

It was simplest to just push it through the doorway and let it bounce down the stoop. Then he dragged it across the lawn, detouring around tree trunks, and out over the wooden dock.

The rowboat was out perpendicular to the dock. Parker pulled it closer with the rope, then pulled on the side until it lay along the edge of the dock. He eased the chair backward until it was lying on its back on the dock, and then tipped it sideways off the edge and into the rowboat. It hit face down, which meant the body hit rather than the wooden chair, which muffled the sound.

Claire's boathouse had a small-wattage bulb hanging from a wire in the middle of the ceiling. Parker switched it on and padded around the concrete edging, gathering up things to weight the body: a length of rusty chain, a broken piece of concrete block, an

199

old metal pulley. He took them all back outside and fixed them around the chair and the body, then tied the rowboat to the rear of the motorboat, and got in the motorboat to tow it out to the middle of the lake.

The toughest part was getting the chair and the body out of the boat. The rowboat bounced and jounced, but wouldn't tip over, and Parker finally had to climb in to it and lift the chair over the side. But then it dropped down into the water at once, and disappeared.

The main thing was, if this area was going to be home base, it had to be kept clean. No sudden unsolved murders, no crime wave of any kind; crooked doings would show up around a rural section like this like a thumbtack under a coat of paint. Which was why replacing the divots took precedence over finding the two in the Corvette.

The rest went pretty fast now, after he sank the body. He towed the rowboat back to the house where he'd borrowed it, and used the bailing can from the motorboat to splash away the bloodstains Morris had left behind. Then he stepped into the cold water himself and scrubbed his body clean, and stood after that by the water's edge while he put his clothes on again over his wet skin.

It was impossible to get the rowboat back into its original position without help from a second man; Parker dragged it close as he could, and left it there. Then he went back to steer the motorboat along to the left, close to shore, and return it to the boathouse he'd taken it from. The kicked-in door was simple vandalism, the normal kind of petty crime in this area and nothing to worry about.

Morris' Plymouth was waiting in the driveway. Parker got in it and drove the long way back to Claire's house, avoiding the highway.

Claire had a mop and a bucket and was doing the kitchen floor. She'd dressed in slacks and sweater and sandals, she'd tied her hair up in a cloth, and she had the fixed look of a woman who is going to make it by will power alone. The table and chairs had already been cleaned and set right, the dishwasher was buzzing, and the few stains that had been along one wall were gone.

Parker came in and said, 'No trouble?'

'No trouble.' The rifle was lying on the kitchen table. Claire saw Parker looking at it, and she said, 'Next time I'll know what to do with that. I learn fast, when I have to.'

'It's loaded again?'

'Of course.'

Parker sat down at the table, pushing the rifle slightly away. 'Tell me about them now. Who they are, what their game is, what their connection is, anything they told you.'

'Morris told most of it. For my benefit, I think. He already knew who they were.'

'What was Morris doing here?'

'He was doing the same thing you were. He'd heard that your friend Keegan was looking for him, so he went to Keegan to find out why. He found this phone number there, so he came here to find out if you knew what was going on.'

'What about the other two?'

'One of them is named Manny Berridge. He's—'

'Berridge?'

'You didn't tell me about the man who was killed. He was supposed to do the robbery with you, wasn't he?'

'That's right. Manny's his son?' That was the one Parker had wounded, the one called Manny.

'Grandson.' She went on to tell him what Morris had said, and he sat and listened to it, frowning at the rifle in front of him on the table.

When she was done, he said, 'What about the other one? Jessup, you say? What's his connection?'

'I don't know. I suppose he's just Manny's friend. He's the brains of the two, but Manny can be much meaner. He's like an insane little child.'

'All right.' He got to his feet, pushing the chair back from the table.

She looked at him, her expression apprehensive. 'You're going after them? But they won't bother us any more, will they?'

'Yes. They strike me as the kind to hold grudges. In the meantime. I want you to do something for me.'

She had finished with the mop, had emptied the bucket into the sink and put mop and bucket both away in the narrow closet in the corner. Now she'd started cleaning the sink. Holding the cleanser in her hand, she said, 'What do you want me to do?'

'Take Morris' Plymouth to New York and lose it.'

'No.' She turned her back and sprinkled cleanser into the sink.

'It's not to get you away from here.'

'It is.' She started scrubbing the sink.

'Partly. The rest is, we can't have the car found around here. In New York it won't raise any questions, but here it would.'

'I'll take it tomorrow.'

'It would be best to do it now, at night.'

She faced him again, leaning against the sink. 'I suppose you're right,' she said, 'but I'm not going to do it. I have something else I have to do first. When I'm finished I'll take the car in, if I'm not too tired.'

'What do you have to do?'

'Get my house back. When I finish here, I have some things to do in the bedroom and the bathroom, and then the porch floor has to be mopped. And then I want to make a list of the people I have to call tomorrow. Someone to fix the glass in the door. Someone to fix the bathroom door.'

He looked at her, and understood vaguely that there was something in her head about the idea of *home* that wasn't in his head and never would be. The world could go to hell if it wanted, but she would put her home in order again before thinking about anything else.

He tried to find something in his own mind to relate that to, so he could understand it better, and the only thing he came up with was betrayal. If someone double-crossed him in a job, tried to take Parker's share of the split or betray him to the law, everything else bacame unimportant until he had evened the score. And like the two tonight, Manny and Jessup; there was no way that Parker was not going to settle with them for the insult of their attack. In some way, what Claire was into now had to be something like that, with a sense of home instead of a sense of identity.

'All right,' he said. 'Just keep the rifle in the same room with you.'

'I will. And this time I won't shoot until I know what I'm shooting at.'

'Good. When I come back, I'll knock twice before I come in. If anybody else walks in without knocking, don't think about it. Just shoot his head off.'

'I will,' she said.

CHAPTER THREE

The Corvette was parked on a gravel strip beside a small white clapboard house across the road from the lake, less than half a mile from Claire's place. Damp blood was on the seat-back on the passenger side.

Parker was on foot, the automatic in his right hand. He was traveling without any kind of light. He circled the house beside the Corvette and found it locked up tight, no sign of entry.

A wooded area stretched away uphill behind the house. Parker considered it, and rejected it, for three reasons: Manny was wounded. Manny and Jessup were both city boys. Jessup would want another car, so he would prefer to stay near houses.

Claire had suggested earlier that Manny and Jessup wouldn't be coming back because they were cowards, and Parker had seen no reason at that point to disagree with her. But cowardice was irrelevant. Whether they were cowards or not, they wouldn't make another attack on the house tonight with an armed man inside and a wounded man outside. And whether they were cowards or not, they would eventually come back to repay Parker for routing them; cowardice would simply at that point make them more difficult to deal with.

Parker didn't know Jessup, had seen him only once and then for only a few seconds of sudden activity, but he felt he understood the man. Jessup was the planner and organizer in his partnership with Manny, just as Parker was the planner and organizer in his own partnerships. So he put himself in Jessup's place now, and decided what Jessup wanted to do and how he'd go about it.

Jessup wanted to get away from here. For that he would need a car. It was now not yet ten o'clock in the evening, and there was nowhere around here that cars were left parked at the curb; there were no curbs here, just the country roads and the houses. The weekenders would be taking their cars away from here tonight, and the fulltime residents wouldn't start settling down for the night for another hour or two. Jessup, when he stole a car, would have to take one from a garage, or at the best, a driveway. In either case, the car would be very close to the owner's home, there might be a dog in the house—people out here tended to have dogs—and the only safe thing to do was wait until very late before making the move.

In the meantime, Jessup had Manny to contend with and Parker to watch out for. So his first move would be to abandon the Corvette just far enough away from Claire's house so that Parker wouldn't be able to see him do it, assuming Parker to have gone down the driveway to watch the Corvette drive away; that much he had done, because here was the Corvette, one road curve away from Claire's house.

Next? Next Jessup would want an empty house to hole up in. He would leave Manny here in the car while he scouted around and found a suitable house, and then he would come back and get Manny and the two of them would go to the house he'd found. And that much he'd done, too, as was evidenced by how much bleeding Manny had done into the Corvette seat-back. All of that hadn't happened in half a mile of driving: one minute, two minutes.

Which meant the empty house had to be nearby. Near enough for Jessup to have gone to it, and come back for Manny, taken Manny to it.

Parker stood beside the Corvette, frowning past the houses across the road at the vaguely seen lake. He was putting himself in Jessup's place, running Jessup's race for him.

Which direction? From here, in which direction would Jessup first look for an empty house in which to hole up?

Back. That was what Parker would do, and he was assuming Jessup would do the same. When being chased, having established the direction you're running in, always double back when you're going to hole up for a while.

Which side of the road? Having put the Corvette over here, would Jessup now choose one of the houses on the lake side of the road? Parker didn't think so, both because of the psychological pressure of Claire's house being on that side and also because Jessup would shy away from resting in a spot where he'd have blocked his own retreat in case of trouble. In this situation Parker would want dry land on all four sides of the place where he was hiding, and he anticipated Jessup would want the same.

It was true that circumstances might have forced Jessup to choose a house somewhere else, but it seemed to Parker that Jessup's first preference would be back in the direction he had come from, on this side of the road.

Parker nodded. He turned away from the Corvette and walked on up behind the white clapboard house and headed back the way he'd come.

CHAPTER FOUR

He knew it was the right house the instant he saw it. It was set farther back from the road than most of the other houses along here, which meant it was built higher on the hillside that sloped up from the lake, and it was a large house, with a second floor and a full attic, which meant that it commanded the best view available of the surrounding area. Sheets of clear plastic had been tacked around all the windows and doors, to protect them from the winter, and the fact they were still in place meant the owners hadn't yet come up to open the house for the summer.

Parker had come along behind the houses, through lawns or gardens or scrub, depending on the ideas of the owner, checking each building out as he had come to it, and this large sprawling stone house was the fifth one from the Corvette, back toward Claire's place. Parker saw it, and knew it was the right one, and cautiously approached it, making a wide circle so as to come down at it from behind, knowing he would be less visible against the woods than with the road or other houses for a backdrop.

And saw light. He stopped when he saw it, because it didn't belong; Jessup wouldn't be stupid enough to turn on lights.

But the other one would. Manny, he would.

The light could very faintly be seen, through a window with plastic sheeting on the outside and a shade pulled all the way down on the inside. Thin lines of yellowish light were revealed where the shade was warped inward away from the window frame.

A very dim light. Parker frowned

downslope at it, and then saw that it was flickering, and realized it was a candle. The electricity wouldn't be on in that house, in any case. There wouldn't be water, either; people around here drained the water from the pipes when they closed their houses for the winter.

Manny must have wanted light, so he could see what damage had been done to his shoulder or arm by Parker's bullet. Jessup had given in to him, taking a chance on the very small light of a candle, in a room at the rear of the house.

But if Jessup were really smart, he wouldn't travel with Manny at all.

Parker moved again, slowly. There was always the chance that the candle was a stunt, that Jessup realized Parker would hunt him down, and had left the candle burning so Parker would move into a position where Jessup could ambush him. It was unlikely, but it was a chance.

A small shedlike addition had been built on at the right rear corner of the house, and that was where Jessup and Manny had gained admission. They had probably tried to neaten up in their wake, to make it impossible to trail them, but there'd been no way for them to reattach the plastic sheeting from the inside, and it sagged crookedly now, open practically all the way up the one side.

Jessup had been more careful with the

door; however he had gotten in, he'd left the door unscarred and managed to lock it again behind him.

Which probably meant the kind of bolt lock that can be opened with a knife blade slipped between door and jamb. Parker took out his own knife, opened it, slid it through, found the bolt, and forced it slowly out of the way, at the same time turning the knob and leaning part of his weight against the door.

It popped open, without a sound.

Parker waited half a minute, then eased the door farther inward, until it bumped against something and there was a faint clinking sound. There was about a four-inch opening now. Parker crouched, put his left hand carefully through the opening, and felt around on the other side of the door for what he'd hit. His fingers brushed cardboard; the clinking sounded again, small and close.

Soda bottles. Two six-pack cartons of empty soda bottles. Jessup, after coming in here, had rooted around and come up with these cartons of empty bottles, which he'd stood one atop the other just inside the door he'd breached. So that if Parker did get this far, he would knock the cartons over when he opened the door: burglar alarm.

Moving carefully in the darkness, with just the one arm reaching around the door, Parker removed the top carton and set it to one side, and then slid the lower carton out of the way.

Was that all? He felt around some more, but as far as he could reach, there was nothing else in the way. He straightened, and cautiously pushed the door open, and there were no other obstructions.

But there was another door. This one, which led from the shed-type annex in to the main part of the house, had apparently given Jessup more trouble; it was obviously breached, with gouged wood protruding from the jamb around the area of the lock.

Because of the empty bottles at the first door, Parker was very slow and careful now, but this door hadn't been booby-trapped at all. Apparently Jessup had placed all his faith in the soda bottles. Or else he'd assumed that a man who would get past them would get past whatever else he might be able to set up at the inner door.

It was two steps up through that inner door, and inside there was unrelieved blackness. Parker moved forward by touch, and could tell he was in a kitchen. Alert for booby traps, planned or inadvertent, he felt his way around the walls till he came to a doorway across from the back entrance, and stepped carefully through there.

Light. Very little, so faint as to be almost nothing at all, and half the time flickering down to *be* nothing at all. But the faintest light is a beacon against complete darkness, and Parker had no trouble seeing it, or moving toward it.

He was in a hall now, a central corridor that ran from the kitchen to the living room at the front of the house, with other rooms opening off on both sides along the way. It was a doorway on the left that showed the flicker of light. Parker moved forward, and when he reached that doorway the light wasn't coming from that room, but from another room beyond it, this being light-spill from light-spill. Diagonally across this room—a kind of library-parlor—was a doorway leading to a room that would be next to the kitchen at the rear of the house; the right spot for the window where he'd first seen the light wobbling.

This library-parlor was carpeted, and the reflected candle-glow made it possible to see the bulks of furniture. Parker moved more quickly across this room, and looked through the doorway into the room with the light.

A small bedroom. A single bed against the rear wall, under the window. A dresser to the right, a wooden chair and a portable television set on a stand to the left.

The candle was stuck in a Chianti bottle on the floor, the bottle covered with the drippings of dozens of previous candles of different colors. This one was red, it was about three inches long, and its light was yellow.

Manny was lying on his back on the bed,

gazing at the ceiling. He was stripped to the waist. His left side was to Parker, and his right shoulder, the one that had been hit, was swathed in ripped sections of sheet, a bulky and awkward bandage, but apparently the best Jessup could do under the circumstances. Manny didn't seem to be in any pain; his expression as he gazed at the ceiling was bland, quiet, pleasant, contented, tentatively interested.

On the floor near the candle in the bottle lay a small crumpled piece of paper. It looked like the piece of paper Parker had found in the empty farmhouse where Briley had been lured.

Jessup wasn't in the room.

Parker squatted on his heels beside the doorway, looking through at Manny, his head just slightly above the level of Manny's head. Jessup wasn't here. Out getting a car? This early? Wait for him here?

Something made a noise upstairs. Whatever had caused it, it became an anonymous thump by the time it reached this corner of the house.

Parker frowned. Which one did he want behind him? It all depended how long Manny would be away on his trip. Jessup was more dangerous in the long run, because he was rational, but Manny could have moments when he would be very bad to be around.

What was Jessup doing up there? Parker

concentrated on that question, and had trouble with it because he would have known better himself than to trap himself away on the second floor. Just as he would have known better than to split his forces. Just as he would have known better than to let Manny trip out now, no matter how much pain Manny might be in.

But he would have known better than to be with Manny anyway.

There was always the tactic of finishing Manny off now, and then going after Jessup. The arguments in favor of it were strong, but two things stopped him. In the first place, he couldn't be sure it could be done quietly enough to keep from alerting Jessup. And in the second place, moving into a lighted room with Jessup on the loose somewhere around didn't appeal to him.

Finally he simply turned away from the lit room and made his way back to the corridor, and then moved cautiously down it looking for the stairs. He was very sensitive to the fact that there was light behind him and none ahead of him; he was outlined for Jessup, if Jessup was in front of him. He stayed as close to the wall as he could get, and moved slowly and silently, straining his eyes to see into the dark. And at the same time, he could feel in his shoulder blades the presence of the man lying on his back in the room with the candle.

The stairs, too, were carpeted. He went up

them close to the wall, and on all fours, to distribute his weight and lessen the chance of creaking. There was still a small hint of light from the candle when he started, but halfway to the top he was in total darkness again.

At the top he halted and listened; Jessup had made one noise, he might make another. But there was no sound, and finally it was time to move.

It total darkness, it was impossible to work out the design of rooms and hallways and doors. Parker simply moved left along the first wall he came to, until he reached a door. He turned the knob, inchingly, and pushed the door open, and saw a vague dim rectangle of slightly paler black: a window. Would this be a bedroom? Would he be standing in a hallway of some kind?

He held his breath, and leaned forward into the room, listening. Men breathe, and in total silence their breathing can be heard. Parker remained leaning forward, with his head and shoulders past the doorway, doing no breathing of his own, until he was sure the room was empty. Then he straightened again, and left the door slightly ajar, and moved past it to continue along the same wall as before.

He checked a second room the same way. The third door he came to opened toward him, and showed no window-rectangle inside. He felt the black air in front of himself and touched shelves, sheets, towels: the linen closet. He pushed the door to without shutting it entirely, and moved on.

A corner. He turned right, came to another doorway, this one with the door standing open. Again, no rectangle of window. He reached forward into the darkness—it was like reaching into black cotton, and feeling nothing—but this time there were no shelves, there was nothing within arm's length at all. He touched the wall to the left of the doorway, on the inside, and found a light switch; so this was a room of some kind. He leaned in, holding his breath again, and it was empty.

But what sort of room was it, and did one or more other rooms lead off it? He had to know. Slowly he crossed the threshold, and the floor felt somehow different beneath his feet. He squatted down, holding the doorjamb, and felt the floor, and it was tile. A bathroom. Not a route then to anywhere else. He straightened, backed out of the doorway, moved on.

Another empty room, and then another corner. If he was working the building plan out in his head properly, the rooms on this side would face the road. Then a fourth side to come, and he should wind up back at the stairs. If he didn't find Jessup first.

Could he be in the attic? Parker hadn't found the stairs going up there yet.

The first room he came to on the third side

217

was occupied. He leaned in and listened, and out of the normal rustle of silence he gradually culled the sound of breathing, faint and regular and quite far away.

There were two vague rectangles of window in this room, and the one on the left seemed more indistinct at the bottom, it didn't have the clarity of line that the one beside it had. As though a piece of furniture were in the way. Or a man.

Jessup was sitting at the window, looking out at the road. Waiting for Parker? Watching one side of the house?

There was the faint odor of cigarette in the air. Jessup had been smoking, too.

Parker straightened, and stepped to one side of the doorway, outside the room. The automatic was in his right hand, but he didn't want to use it unless he had to. The broken door in the kitchen of this house would be vandalism, and cause no unusual concern. Blood in any of the rooms would attract the wrong kind of attention.

Parker inhaled and exhaled. Holding the breath altered the responses of the muscles, just slightly. He leaned against the wall for a minute, breathing normally, and then turned and stepped silently in through the doorway.

The indistinctness at the bottom of the left window was still there. Parker moved toward it, taking small steps on carpeting, feeling in front of himself with one hand at every step.

'Manny? That you?'

The voice seemed very sudden. Parker froze where he was, one arm extended downward and out in front of himself, back bent slightly, right heel lifted.

Some people are very sensitive to the presence of another person in the same room. Jessup's attention hadn't been entirely on the nothing happening down below on the road; he had sensed Parker's presence.

Parker stayed where he was, waiting for Jessup to decide he'd made a mistake. He continued to breathe, but slowly, with long silent intakes and exhalations.

The darkness shifted, at the bottom of the left window. It now matched the right window, squared off bottom and top.

'Manny! He's up here!' A loud shout, for the benefit of the one downstairs, lying on that bed. And Jessup didn't sound worried, it was simply a shouted bit of information.

Parker moved during the sound of Jessup's shout; he backed toward the doorway, holding his left hand out behind him. He stopped when Jessup's voice stopped.

Silence. And then, belatedly, a sleepy shout back, a query from below, with no intelligible words.

'He's up here with me!' Parker moved backward. He would not let himself be between Jessup and the windows, he would not be outlined. Jessup wouldn't have the same reluctance to use a gun.

This time Jessup kept shouting, giving Parker time to get all the way back to the door, and take one step to the left of it, within the room, and stand there with his back to the wall, the doorway just past his right elbow.

Jessup shouted, 'Put out the light! Get to the bottom of the stairs and wait for him, in case he gets away from me!'

Would Manny do it? Or would Manny just prop himself on his elbow on the bed and gaze blearily at the doorway in the candlelight, and gradually just sink down again and forget all about it?

There were no more answers from downstairs, only the first muffled question. Jessup didn't shout any more instructions; either he was sure Manny would do what he was told, or he wanted Parker to think he was. In either case, Manny's one return shout had told Jessup that Manny was still alive and all right, that Parker had not already taken him out of the play.

Everybody was silent for a while now. Parker had kept his eyes on the smudgy rectangles of the windows. Jessup had been in front of the one on the left, and had disappeared from that one without having gone past the one on the right. Which meant that Jessup was somewhere in the left side of the room. Coming this way? Staying in one spot?

If he were going to get out of the room, he had two choices. He could either work his way around the wall, in which case he would run into Parker just before he reached the door, or he could get down on hands and knees and crawl to the door, in which case there was the slight possibility that he would get by Parker; but it was very slight. And in any case, Parker was getting to know Jessup better now, and he had the feeling Jessup wouldn't crawl to the door. Just as he wouldn't have gone up the stairs on all fours, though that was the best way to do it.

Jessup was half-good, which is the other side of being half-assed. He knew how to do some things right, but he wasn't careful enough, he didn't follow through on the reasons for doing this or that or the other. He would be one of those people who live their lives as a movie, in which they star and direct and write the story. That kind goes for drama, like traveling with a Manny. Or the way they handled Keegan. Or what they did to Claire with Morris' body. And a man like that won't crawl across a floor to a doorway, not if his life depends on it.

That was the edge Parker had; he knew that survival was more important than heroics. It isn't how you play the game, it's whether you win or lose.

CHAPTER FIVE

A wristwatch with a radium dial. Parker looked at it, a faint green circle swimming in the darkness over there, and waited for the time it counted to make Jessup do something stupid.

Stupid like the watch.

They had been stalemated for about ten minutes now. Jessup had spoken once, seven or eight minutes ago, saying, 'Don't try to convince me you aren't here. I know you are.' But at that time he hadn't shifted so that the radium dial was showing yet, so Parker hadn't moved while he'd talked, simply looked at the place the voice was coming from, to know where Jessup was.

It was in the same area that the green circle, two or three minutes after that, swam to the surface. Whatever position Jessup was standing in, it pointed that circle directly at Parker. Occasionally the thing dove back into the darkness, as Jessup moved—silently—one way or another, shifting position, but it always came back again, and Parker watched it, and waited for Jessup to do something stupid.

It would have a sweep second hand, that watch. By now Jessup would be feeling every second.

There had been no further sound or movement from downstairs. Had Manny heard Jessup? Had he done what Jessup wanted, or had he smiled and nodded and stayed lying there on the bed? Or was he coming upstairs, slowly so as not to make any noise, to find out what was going on? Parker's right elbow extended into the doorway area, to warn him if anyone tried to move in or out.

From the location of the green circle swimming there, Jessup wasn't against a wall. Unless he had a piece of furniture to lean on, he would be feeling tired by now.

'You still there, Parker? It is Parker, isn't it?'

Parker took a sliding step forward while Jessup talked. He stopped when Jessup was silent.

The silence this time lasted no more than thirty seconds. 'You're the last one, you know that?' Jessup was trying to sound cocky and humorous, but he was nerved up and the sound of it was in his voice. 'Did you see what we did to your friend Keegan? And Morris? Briley's dead in the woods someplace, did you know that?'

Parker had covered half the distance to the watch; simultaneously, Jessup stopped talking and the watch disappeared. Parker stayed where he was.

The watch came back, disappeared again, came back again. Jessup was gesturing while

223

he talked, making gestures in the dark. 'You don't fool me, I know you're in this room. I can *feel* you. What do you think I am, a punk like Manny? A punk like you people?'

Parker was almost close enough to touch him. Another pace. Jessup was silent, and Parker stood there, looking forward into the darkness, knowing Jessup's head was just *there*, a few inches beyond arm's reach. He waited.

Was Jessup finished talking? Parker breathed shallowly through his nose; the automatic was away in its holster under his left arm, but his right hand hovered near it, in case things turned that way.

'You want to wait till daylight. That's okay with—'

Parker's left hand touched shirt, snaked upward, the fingers closed around throat. His right hand came around, closed, and when he hit he felt Jessup's teeth against his knuckles.

Jessup was making a high gargling sound, and thrashing like a spider stuck through with a pin. Parker hit him again, holding him in place with the left hand around Jessup's neck, hitting at the face in the darkness.

Fingers crawled along Parker's left arm, hurrying toward his head. Parker stepped in close and brought his knee up and felt it hit. But Jessup wrapped his arms around Parker's waist and lunged forward, and his weight forced Parker to take a backward step. His shin hit something, a chair or table or part of a bed, and his balance was gone, and the two of them toppled over through darkness and hit the floor.

Parker's first grip was lost. He couldn't let Jessup get free, he had to know where he was. He slapped outward, and touched cloth, and clung to it. Hands punched at him, they both shifted and rolled on the floor, their feet kicking at anonymous pieces of furniture, and suddenly they rolled directly into one another and both grabbed for leverage and control.

It was weight that made the difference. Parker was a little heavier, a little stronger, a little more sure of himself. He had Jessup's throat again with one hand, and one of Jessup's wrists with the other, and he was slowly forcing Jessup onto his back, pushing him backward and over and down. Jessup's free hand punched out, the punches growing both wilder and frailer, and Parker tucked his head down to protect his face and bore Jessup steadily backward, and down, and flattened him on the floor. Then knelt on the wrist he'd been holding, freeing his other hand. But this time didn't waste effort with fists; he put the second hand with the first, on Jessup's throat, and clamped them there, and wouldn't move.

Jessup kicked, and clawed with his free hand at the fingers around his throat, and scratched at Parker's face and neck and arms. Parker knelt over him, one knee on Jessup's wrist, the other leg stretched out behind himself for balance, and leaned his weight on his arms, outstretched, a straight line from his shoulders to Jessup's throat, the weight of his body and the tightness of his grip pinning Jessup in place and holding the breath from his lungs.

Light. Orange-gray, faint, flickering. Parker saw it reflected in Jessup's bulging eyes, and looked up to see the doorway framed with orange-yellow light, and then Manny padded forward into the doorway, barefoot, wearing only his slacks, carrying in his unwounded left hand the Chianti bottle with the candle in it, and in his right hand—despite the wound in that shoulder—a small pistol; it looked like a .22, a ladies' purse gun.

Manny was smiling. His face seemed to flicker like the candlelight, his eyes grew larger and smaller, and moisture on his chin reflected the light like chrome.

If he'd been feeling anything at all, he wouldn't have been able to hold the gun like that, or bend his arm like that.

His voice was very gentle, lamblike, the sweet child: 'Let him go.'

226

CHAPTER SIX

At first, Parker didn't move. Jessup was weakening beneath him, it would be a help to have at least one of them out of the play. He looked back at Manny, standing there in the doorway, and from the corners of his eyes he tried to find something to throw. To get rid of the light. In the darkness, they'd be more equal.

But there was nothing. This was a teenager's bedroom—from the walls, rock posters gyrated in the candlelight—and the center of the floor was empty. A chair and small table that had been nearby were now kicked away into the corner by the bed, leaving nothing close enough to reach in a single lunge.

'Bang bang,' said Manny gently. He made a small lifting motion with the gun barrel. Get up, he was saying, or be shot where you are.

Parker moved, very slowly, shifting his weight back to his knees from his hands, but keeping the fingers clamped tight around Jessup's throat till the last second. Jessup's eyes were rounding out from his head, filming over. His hands had fallen to the floor on either side of his head. His legs were moving, but without purpose, like a dog when he dreams in his sleep.

227

Parker released him at last, and leaned back on his haunches. He kept watching Manny, because Manny was the danger now, but he remained aware of Jessup, who at first didn't change his position, just continued to lie there on his back with his legs twitching. Then Jessup made a loud harsh grinding noise in his throat, and his whole body flopped like a fish: air, finding its way back into his body again.

Manny smiled sweetly at Jessup, as though Jessup had just done something cute and clever for his benefit. 'There we are,' he said. 'You're all right now.'

But Jessup wasn't all right. His own hands were at his throat now, and his mouth was open wide. His eyes still bulged, and his face was still mottled dark, and his tongue was still too thick in his mouth. Parker's weight leaning on him like that had done him some damage; the regular channel for air was at least partially blocked.

Parker slowly moved the leg on the side opposite Manny, lifting the knee and getting his foot under himself, so he'd have more impetus if he had to make a sudden movement anywhere. Manny was concentrating most of his attention on Jessup now, and Parker kept the rest of his body still, his face turned toward Manny, his arms hanging down at his sides.

Manny's expression, dulled and stupid-looking and childish, was gradually shifting from the smile of happiness to a puzzled frown. He said 'Jessup? You *are* okay, aren't you?'

Jessup went on making the sounds. They were like dry heaves, only worse.

'We'd better get you a doctor,' Manny said. He was the follower, and the idea of losing his leader terrified him. 'We'd better get you a doctor right away.'

Parker's left foot was on the floor now, and he lifted his left hand and rested it on his knee.

Manny frowned at Parker. 'I ought to shoot you,' he said poutingly. 'I ought to shoot you in the balls.'

'You couldn't carry him,' Parker said. 'And he can't walk. And you want to get him to a doctor.'

Manny's frown deepened; he was working his way through the brambles of what Parker had said. '*You* carry him,' he said. 'That's better, you can help fix things again. You pick him up and carry him.'

Parker reached down and slid one arm under Jessup's shoulders and one under his knees.

Manny said, 'And you be careful with him. If you hurt him, I'll hurt you.'

Parker lifted Jessup into his arms, and then got to his feet. Jessup was still making the noises, but with long dry spaces of silence between them; then another grinding rasping intake of breath, and silence, and another tearing abrasive exhalation.

Manny backed out of the doorway as Parker approached him. Parker turned sideways to get Jessup through the doorway, and Manny moved back and to his left and gestured for Parker to go first down the stairs.

Jessup's breathing started to get easier on the way down. With Manny three or four steps behind him, with no light but the candle, it was possible for Parker to reach his left hand around and close it over Jessup's windpipe again. But this time he didn't want Jessup dead, not yet. Jessup's life was protecting his own right now. He simply didn't want Jessup improving.

Manny was cautious and alert, within his limitations, but his limitations were severe. Parker had three chances at him before they left the house, going out the same back door they'd all entered by, but he didn't want to take over from Manny yet. Manny didn't know it, but he was helping Parker solve his problems.

The next step Manny came to on his own, without suggestions: 'We'll take your car,' he said when they'd gone outside. He blew out the candle and threw the Chianti bottle away; it hit grass, and didn't break. 'You're the son of a bitch, this is all your fault, we can take your car.'

Parker led the way, carrying Jessup, and Manny followed. It was less dark out here, and only sporadically could Parker close off Jessup's air supply. But it was enough; whatever damage had been done, Parker could do enough now to keep it from correcting itself.

There was a driveway beside the house. They walked down it to the road and turned right. There were no houses showing light along this stretch, and looking between houses and out across the lake, Parker saw only two or three lights from over there. It was around eleven now; most of the weekenders had already gone, and the locals were starting to bed down for the night.

The only lights they saw on this side of the lake were those at Claire's house, when they'd walked around the curve. Manny was keeping ten or fifteen feet back, and his feet scuffed when he walked. Parker didn't know exactly what he'd taken, but it seemed to serve mostly as a sort of super-tranquilizer. It wasn't LSD, which was simply a sledgehammer that took you away and brought you back again, but it was a chemical of a similar kind. In any case, it was taken in a similar way, injected into a sugar cube and then the sugar cube sucked and swallowed. Some kind of speed, maybe, STP, the stuff that does permanent brain damage; *Speed Kills*, the warnings had said in the underground press. In any case, it was a stuff that didn't take him away completely, and didn't bring him back complete. It put an erratic cog in the engine of his brain; it would soon burn the engine out, but in the meantime its running would be wild and unpredictable.

At Claire's house, a light showed in the kitchen window. If Manny wanted to go in there again, Parker would have to take care of him here; he would prefer to take it all away from this neighborhood first.

The kitchen light glinted on the Plymouth, Morris' car. Parker headed for it, and behind him Manny said, 'That's yours?'

'I have the keys to it.'

Parker opened the rear door and laid Jessup across the back seat. He got out again and closed the door and turned to look at Manny.

Manny said, 'Goodbye.'

'You can't drive with that arm,' Parker said.

Manny frowned, and glanced down at his arm. He looked back at Parker, and his expression was uncertain again.

Parker said, 'And Jessup wouldn't want you to kill me yet. Or let me go.'

Manny grinned disbelievingly, though his larger puzzlement still showed through. 'You think I'm going to let you drive?'

232

'You can't. And I know where to find a doctor.'

'How come you're so eager?'

'I want to stay alive a while longer.'

Manny frowned deeply, thinking about it. He glanced at the house, and Parker saw him thinking about phoning a doctor from here. Then he glanced at the Plymouth, and Parker knew he was imagining Jessup giving him orders. He wasn't used to doing the planning himself.

Parker said, 'You're wasting time. But he's your friend, not mine.'

It was being used to taking orders, having somebody else do the thinking, that decided it. Manny looked at him and said, 'I'll be in the back seat. I'll be right behind you. You do anything funny, I'll shoot you in the back of the head.'

'I know that.'

'All right,' Manny said.

CHAPTER SEVEN

The eastbound traffic was as heavy as ever, moving along bumper to bumper at a steady thirty-five miles an hour. Parker forced his way between a Ford station wagon and a Rambler sedan, and settled down to drive.

He couldn't see Manny in the rear-view mirror, but he could sense him back there, in the left side of the rear seat. He had Jessup's head in his lap, his wounded right arm was draped down across Jessup's chest, and the .22 was in his left hand.

The incredible thing was, he hadn't disarmed Parker. Probably because Parker had been using his hands instead of a gun, Manny must have decided there wasn't any gun in it at all. Parker felt it, against his left side, and drove steadily along behind the Ford, the Rambler's headlights in his rear-view mirror.

He didn't know exactly how he was going to work all this out with Manny and Jessup, only that he wanted to get the two of them—and this car—as far as possible from Colliver Pond. The Plymouth had Ohio plates; ten or fifteen miles should be far enough away.

And after that there'd be nothing to take care of but the Corvette. Buy one new tire, use the spare for the other, and Claire could drive it to New York tomorrow and leave it there. Parker's own car, the Pontiac, had to be picked up from the other side of the lake. Then everything would be neat again.

But first Manny and Jessup had to be taken care of. In one way Manny was better to operate against, because he could be conned and dazzled, but Manny wasn't entirely rational, his reactions couldn't be counted on as Jessup's could. Parker knew that at any

234

second it might enter Manny's head to start shooting, regardless of the fact that Parker was at the wheel and they were traveling at thirty-five miles an hour in all this traffic, regardless of any reasonable consideration at all. He couldn't help it, his shoulders remained hunched, he felt he was holding his head stiffly, as though if he tensed sufficiently, the bullets would bounce off him.

Jessup had grown quiet again, and that might complicate matters, too, if he recovered sufficiently to take over giving orders. He would want Parker disposed of right away, and he wouldn't want a doctor.

Parker glanced at the speedometer. They'd come four miles from the turnoff. He would go ten miles, and then take the first likely-looking side road.

'How far to this doctor?' Manny sounded more irritable, less tranquilized. The nervousness in the situation must be counteracting the acid.

'Five or six more miles,' Parker said. 'It won't be long.'

'He's the closest doctor?'

'He's the closest safe doctor,' Parker said. 'You want a doctor that'll call the cops?'

'Don't worry, nobody's gonna call the cops. You go to the nearest doctor.'

'That means finding a phone book somewhere and looking it up. This is the only

235

doctor I know. We'll be there in ten minutes, maybe less.'

'Why don't you pass some of these people?' Manny was getting increasingly irritable. He was coming down off his high, and his wounded arm was probably bothering him, particularly because of the way he'd been overworking it.

'After this curve,' Parker said. He too was impatient. They'd come seven miles now.

In the next two miles, he managed to pass three cars. It made no difference in the timing, three car lengths wasn't any great distance, but it made Manny feel better to think they were hurrying.

Nine miles. In the back seat, Jessup had started moaning, and moving around. Parker listened, his head back a bit so he could hear better, his eyes frequently on the rear-view mirror.

Ten miles. Motion in the mirror; Manny's head lowering. They were whispering together back there, either because Jessup had no voice now or because he was telling Manny how to handle the killing of Parker.

Parker's right hand moved nearer the gun under his left arm.

Again, motion in the mirror, this time Manny's head coming back up. Parker tensed, waiting. There was no traffic coming the other way right now; if necessary, he would throw the car into a swerve to the left and ram a pole or a tree or a house on the other side, and finish them in the confusion. But that was the riskiest way, other ways would be better.

'Stop the car.' Manny's voice, nervousness very plain in it now.

Eleven miles. Parker said, 'The turnoff's just ahead.'

A harshly whispered sentence from Jessup. Manny said, 'All right. Stop after you make the turn.'

It was nearly a mile farther before a road appeared on the right. Parker made the turn, and accelerated hard.

'Stop now.'

'The doctor's just ahead.'

Parker drove at the top speed the road would allow. It was narrow and winding and hilly, a blacktop county road through alternating stretches of woods and cleared farmland. Parker slued around curves and floored the accelerator on the straightaways. Manny might be the kind of fool who didn't think about consequences, but Jessup wasn't, and would know better than to have the driver killed at this kind of speed on this kind of road.

'What the hell you doing? Slow down!' Manny sounded startled and angry, but not really afraid.

'I want to get you to the doctor.' Parker had the high beams on, and he kept staring

237

ahead for a useful place. He knew that Jessup was conscious back there now, he knew that Jessup didn't want any doctor, and he knew that Manny had been told to put a bullet in Parker's head the second the car came to a stop. So it couldn't be done quietly after all.

And there it was. The Plymouth topped a rise and started down the other side, and ahead was a long straightaway, sloping down, with a sharp right at the bottom. And at the curve, directly ahead of the Plymouth, was a broad low concrete-block building painted white, with several plate-glass windows across the front, and with a large sign running the width of the building above the windows, white letters on red: SUSSEX COUNTY TRACTOR SALES, INC. On the stretch of gravel between the front of the building and the road stood several pieces of farm or construction machinery, all painted yellow: tractors, backhoes, bulldozers. At both front corners of the graveled area, on high poles, floodlights glared down on the face of the building and the squatting bulky machinery.

The Plymouth hit ninety going down the straight stretch. In the mirror, Parker saw Jessup struggling upward, his face twisted with strain. Jessup knew something was going to happen, and he wanted to be able to stop it. His voice creaked without intelligible words, and Parker saw the curve coming; he braced his forearms across the steering wheel, pressed his back into the seat back, and slammed his foot down hard on the brakes.

The car bucked, nose down, and squealed forward along the road, the tail swerving bumpily to the left, the rear tires leaving broad stripes of burned-off rubber on the blacktop. Jessup and Manny were flung forward off the seat, and Parker was pressed flat to the steering wheel.

The curve. Parker's left hand was on the door handle; his right foot lifted from the brake, his right hand spun the wheel to the left. The car shook itself and straightened out, pointing at all that yellow machinery. There was a narrow ditch straight ahead; the driveway entrance was farther to the left. Parker pushed down on the door handle, and as the front tires left the road, sailing into the air out over the ditch, he shoved the door open and lunged out, pushing back with his right foot on the accelerator as he went.

The car leaped away, hurdling the ditch. The door slammed behind him, missing his right foot by an inch. The Plymouth bounced on the gravel, sideswiped a backhoe, and ran head-on into the side of a tractor.

CHAPTER EIGHT

Parker's legs hit a tractor tire while he was still rolling; his momentum slued him halfway around before he stopped, on his back in front of the tractor, his legs twisted sideways and knees bent around the tire.

The final crash of the car happened after that, a second or two later. It sounded very loud, and various, as though a dozen cars were involved instead of just one, and the noise seemed to come from everywhere and not from any particular point.

Parker straightened his legs, and felt pain in both of them. He sat up and stroked his palms down over his shins and felt nothing broken, but both would be bruised and aching for a while.

He didn't mind using the automatic here. He took it out, and used the grill of the tractor to help him get up. The legs didn't hurt any more or less when he put weight on them.

The car wasn't burning. That was all right, but he would have preferred a fire. He moved through the machinery toward it, watching. Both headlights were out, and the engine had stopped running.

Parker came around the side of a bulldozer, with the Plymouth directly in front of him, broadside, and the rear door on this side swung open and Jessup fell out, his arm stretched out in front of him, his finger squeezing the trigger of the gun he had pointed at Parker. Ricochets twanged from the yellow metal of the bulldozer, and Parker fired once, then ducked back out of sight, crouching behind a foot-wide tire as high as his shoulder. From high to the right came the glaring light of the floodlights.

'God damn you! God damn you!' It sounded like a frog croaking in words, not like a human voice at all.

Parker moved forward just enough to see. Jessup was kneeling beside the car, gun in his fist, head turning back and forth as he looked for Parker. Behind him, Manny crouched on the floor of the Plymouth, peering out. His face was bloody, and his wounded right arm hung motionless at his side.

Jessup said something in his new raspy voice, speaking to Manny, whose response was sluggish and dull; he backed away deeper into the car, hunching backward without the help of his hurt arm, and Jessup reached out with his free hand and slammed the door. Parker leaned forward to try a shot at him, but Jessup was keyed up now, his senses hyper-alert, and he saw the movement and fired at it, and Parker ducked back again.

Parker was too impatient to live with a stalemate. In front of the tire on the bulldozer

241

was a metal plate, a step for the operator getting up into the seat. Parker stepped up on that, and leaned forward with his elbows on the seat, and looked down over the back of the bulldozer at the Plymouth. At first he could only see the top of the car, but when he hunched farther forward he could see Jessup.

And Jessup saw him. His head and gun-hand flashed up, his eyes staring, and Parker leaned back again, hearing the musical note as the bullet bounced off the machine, feeling the vibration run through the metal.

Was it going to be stalemate after all? Parker stepped back down to the gravel, and headed around the front of the bulldozer to the other side, moving fast despite the troubles in his legs.

Jessup was gone. Parker stepped out into the open, and the Plymouth stood there silent and alone. Manny must still be inside, crouched on the floor in back, but Jessup was somewhere in all this floodlit yellow machinery.

Manny could wait, again. It was Jessup that had to be taken care of first.

Parker stepped back beside the bulldozer and got down awkwardly onto the ground, his legs bothering him. He lay flat on his stomach and turned his head slowly back and forth, looking under all the vehicles, his view obstructed here and there by tires, but most of the graveled area open to him.

242

Nothing. Either Jessup was standing where a tire was between him and Parker, or he was up on one of the machines.

Parker got up again, having more trouble than before—his legs were tightening up on him, soon he wouldn't be able to travel at more than a limping walk at all—and climbed heavily up onto the bulldozer once more. He looked out across the tops of the machines, and still saw nothing.

Jessup had to be around. From here Parker could see the road, and the fields on both sides of the floodlit area, and the front of the building. Jessup hadn't had time to get fully away, even if he'd wanted to leave. And he wouldn't want to get away. He'd want to stay near his partner, and he'd want to kill Parker.

Parker waited, up on the bulldozer step, scanning all the machinery under the lights. He'd outwaited Jessup before, he could do it again. Or had Jessup learned from that?

A wailing sound rose and fell. A banshee sound, a noise for something in a swamp to make when it's near death.

Parker stayed where he was, on the side of the bulldozer, aching right foot on the step, left forearm on the seat, right hand with the gun in it resting on the yellow metal hood. He looked around, and the sound came again, louder than before, and when he looked to his left, the Plymouth was moving. It rocked slightly on its springs, and when it did, the

243

smashed front end scraped against the tractor it had rammed. Small pieces of glass fell to the gravel.

Manny? Was that sound coming from him? Parker leaned over the seat and waited and watched.

After the two wails, there was silence for about a minute, and then a sudden huge shriek, violent and explosive and drawn out. Then silence, this time for less than a minute, and another shriek, and silence again.

Jessup's new voice called, 'Parker! Parker, listen to me!'

Manny shrieked again, and the Plymouth rocked back and forth, the metal of the car squealing against the metal of the tractor.

Jessup called, 'Give me a truce! I've got to help him! Parker?'

There was a little silence, and then Manny yelled, 'No!' And then, 'No, I can't!'

'Parker, for Christ's sake, he took too much, I have to help him!'

'*No!*' Manny yelled. '*No, I can't do that, I can't do that, no no no, I can't do that, the wings, I can't do that, no! I can't, I can't, I can't do that, NO-NO-NO-NO-NO!*'

'Parker! I've got to trust you, I can't let him stay there like that!'

Parker waited, and Jessup came out from the yellow machines, looking this way and that, the gun still in his hand as he hurried toward the Plymouth, where Manny was

244

shrieking again without words.

And that was the difference. Parker shot him twice.

CHAPTER NINE

Manny was lunging around on his back inside the car, arching his body, slamming himself into the floor and the door handles, breaking himself to pieces. Four sugar wrappers lay on the seat.

Parker reached his arm in through the open side window, close enough to leave powder marks, and pulled the trigger. Manny fell still, his broken arms dropping onto his chest. Parker smeared his palms over the automatic and dropped it in on top of the body. The law could work out whatever theory it wanted: a car with Ohio plates, two dead bodies and one of them broken up and full of acid, both shot with the same gun and the gun in the car with one of the corpses, the other one carrying a second gun which had also been fired. They could work out whatever theory they wanted, but none of it would involve Mrs. Claire Willis at Colliver's Pond.

Parker turned and walked away. From the knees down, his legs felt like logs, heavy and unresponsive and aching. He limped badly as he walked back toward the main road.

About a mile up the main road, he remembered, there was a roadside snack bar, on the westbound side of the road, across from all the traffic. He would walk up to there and call Claire to come down and pick him up.

Except he didn't have to. He limped out to the main road, trotted awkwardly across at a break in the traffic, and had walked about a quarter-mile when one of the few westbound vehicles, a farmer's pickup truck, came to a stop beside him, and a gnarled old man with huge-knuckled hands on the steering wheel called out to him, 'You want a lift?'

Parker climbed into the truck, and the farmer started off again, saying, 'You don't want to walk with legs like that.'

'No, I don't. Thanks.'

'Shrapnel? You get it in the war?'

'No,' Parker said. 'I had an accident.'

'I got a bullet in the leg myself,' the old man said. 'During World War One, you know. Still bothers me in the spring.'

CHAPTER TEN

Claire was putting a log on the fire. Parker walked into the living room and she looked at him and said, 'What happened to your legs?'

'I banged them up. They'll be okay.'

246

She straightened from the fireplace and stood looking at him, wiping her hands together. 'Is it finished?'

'They won't be back,' he said. There were no lamps lit in the room, only the fire for illumination; it made Parker think of candlelight, and the muscles in his back tensed. He thought of switching on the lights, but he knew she'd done this for the romantic effect, and he didn't want to spoil it for her. It was easier for him to get over things than for her.

She went over and sat on the sofa and waved to him to join her, saying, 'It is a nice house, isn't it?'

'Yes, it is.' He sat beside her and slowly stretched out his legs, and looked into the fire.

Photoset, printed and bound in Great Britain by REDWOOD PRESS LIMITED, Melksham, Wiltshire